HOUS

HOUSE OF BROKEN DREAMS

a tale of a
Family of Virginia

BYRD ROBERTS

GLB Publishers　　　　　　　　San Francisco

FIRST EDITION
Copyright © 2003 by Byrd Roberts
All rights reserved. Printed in the U.S.A.

No part of this publication may be reproduced or transmitted in any form or by any means, electronic or mechanical, including photocopy, recording or any information storage and retrieval system now known or to be invented, without permission in writing from the publisher, except by a reviewer who wishes to quote brief passages in connection with a review written for inclusion in a magazine, newspaper or broadcast.

Published in the United States by
GLB Publishers
P.O. Box 78212, San Francisco, CA 94107 USA

Cover by W. L. Warner

This is a work of fiction. Other than Alexander Campbell, who was actually one of Norfolk's first aldermen, names, characters, places, and incidents are either the products of the author's imagination or are used fictitiously, and any resemblance to actual persons, living or dead, events, or locales is entirely coincidental.

Library of Congress Control Number:

2003100748

1-879194-41-4

Printed 2003

Byrd Roberts, a retired teacher, was educated at East Carolina University and Duke University. He lives and writes in Ocean View in Norfolk, Virginia.

*Dedicated
to
Lee and David*

CHAPTER ONE

As we were about to leave our dormitory room, Vic noticed a telegram had been slipped under our door. He picked it up.
"It's yours, Mister Strutwick Widdicombe Hall." He grinned and handed it to me. "From one of your admirers, I guess!"
"Not everyone is attracted to red-heads," I parried.
"Oh, I'm not attracted to all red-headed men." Vic teased. "Only those with *dark* red hair and no freckles.... Big blue eyes certainly help, too!"
Vic put an arm around my shoulders while I removed the telegram from its envelope. As I read the contents, my carefree mood vanished.
"It's from Mrs. O'Brian, our housekeeper."
"What is it, Strut? You look so strange."
"My father died today...I'm to return to Norfolk immediately."
I felt lost. Vic pulled me close. Resting my head on his protective chest, my dominant feeling was numbness. My father and I had never been close; we had merely tolerated each other. His death, however, would throw the family into a state of disorder.
"It'll be all right, Strut. You will see." Vic massaged the back of my neck as he spoke. "I will be at your side through all this."
For moments I remained still in his arms. Then, slowly, I disengaged myself and stood straight. "1 guess 1970 isn't turning out to be such a wonderful year," I said grimly. "I wonder what happened to Oliver. A car accident? Whatever, it had to be sudden."
"I'll be in Norfolk by Friday evening, Strut."
"I wouldn't have anything, actually, if I didn't have you, Vic. You come first." Reaching up on tiptoe to kiss him lightly on the cheek, my eyes moistened.
I packed my suitcases while Vic went to gas up my Jaguar. Leaving him there at college was difficult to do. When he returned, he had coffee and sandwiches for us. We ate quickly and then packed the car.
Driving down Interstate Sixty-four gave me time to think.

Victor Gilmore and I had become close back in our prep school days. A bond had been forged between us. I was very much in love with him, thriving on his companionship, reveling in his handsomeness, and adoring his magnificent body. At six foot one, he was four inches taller than I was. His bright brown eyes and good-looking face were crowned with a mass of unruly dark hair. His body was muscular and athletic.

Our families approved of our longstanding "friendship." His family had the money; mine had the esteemed and glorious name. The Widdicombe Family had been in Norfolk forever.

There was little traffic on the interstate, and I made good time. My mind turned to the family. I wondered how Claire was holding up. Smiling, I remembered how she had always discouraged me from calling her Mother. Meek Claire, who had always blended into the background, saying little, seldom smiling. Yet, she wasn't the quiet, efficient type. Claire had always been...simply there. She was accustomed to being cared for all her life.

Well, Mrs. O'Brian was comforting her tonight. I could rely on that. Mrs. O'Brian was loyal to the Widdicombes, and she would be until the day she drew her last breath. She had been with the family for forty years, living in and managing the household, rearing my sister, Carolyn, and me.

The car was stuffy, and I lowered my window a bit. The chilly air was invigorating.

Carolyn. I couldn't be sure how my sister was holding up. She was thirty-five, fifteen years older than I. I realized I did not know her very well. The difference in our ages was a barrier between us, and neither of us had ever tried to overcome it. She was absorbed with her own family...her dear Owen and their three boys. God, I hoped Carolyn hadn't descended on the house with her entire brood. That would overwhelm Claire, who was better left in Mrs. O'Brian's capable hands.

Claire and my father. I tried to think of them as a couple, as a pair, but I couldn't. My father, Oliver Hall, had been cool and self-confident, always so assertive. He had been so much the master of the house that one would have thought he was the Widdicombe, not Claire.

He was gone now, dead at fifty-nine. Whatever had happened

must have been unexpected. Claire would have written me if my father had been taken ill. The bank would feel the loss. Oliver Hall had been a pillar of Norfolk's financial community.

At twenty I was not really prepared to take charge as head of the family. I was intelligent enough to understand that, yet there was no one else to do it. Certainly Claire could not.

I wanted to return to Lexington with Vic in January. I could not endure separation from him now. Perhaps I could organize the household's operation so that I could manage it and go to Washington and Lee, too. Mrs. O'Brian would help me the best she could. Vic would help, also, I was confident.

Then I remembered my great-aunt...Aunt Charlotte. I had never seen her in my life. Months would pass without my even remembering her up there on the third floor. Incredible. Her few needs were seen to by Mrs. O'Brian. The old lady had turned eighty-seven this past October; I remembered Claire saying so, just a single statement of fact not elaborated on. No one in the Widdicombe family ever talked about Aunt Charlotte. There had always been a rule of silence in regard to her. I do not think my father had ever seen her, either.

As a child I had been forbidden to go to the third floor. Once, when I was eleven, I had secretly slipped up the stairs and had listened at her door. Hearing nothing, I slowly turned the knob, but the door was locked from the inside. I was certain it had remained locked to this day.

So, I had the responsibility of Claire and Aunt Charlotte. Younger men than I have had to shoulder family responsibilities. I did feel equal to it, but I was reluctant.

I drove the car into the Hampton Roads tunnel, slowing down to the speed of the cars ahead of me. The tunnel was dank, and its smell irritated my nostrils. When I drove out the exit, I was relieved; returning to Norfolk always made me feel good. I was back on familiar ground.

My headlights immediately blurred into fog wafting through the dark streets. When I turned into the Freemason section of the city, I remembered Claire once told me its former name had been Old Atlantic City. I had wondered at the time if New Jersey had the new one.

Once my Jag turned onto the old cobblestone streets, I had to slow it to a crawl or damage the shocks. Then I saw our house and felt strong. Whatever the situation inside those walls, I would deal with it.

I drove into the carriage house, long ago converted into a garage, and, bags in hand, walked down the brick path and into the walled garden at the rear of the house. When I entered through the French doors to the family dining room, Mrs. O'Brian came from the kitchen to meet me.

Dropping my luggage, I hugged her. She patted my shoulder, meaning to comfort me.

"Mister Strutwick, I hope you're ready for the worst. It's been a mighty bad day for the family."

She looked older. Worry and concern shoved in her green eyes and in the creases on her face. Gone was her usual autocratic demeanor. I had never seen her so devoid of self-confidence.

"Stay calm, and we will work through this together," I said, turning to sit at the dining room table. She touched my arm and stopped me, then gestured toward the chair at the head of the table. "I would like a bourbon and water before we begin, Mrs. O'Brian. Won't you have a drink with me? I imagine you need one, too."

"No, sir, I will not drink with the Widdicombes," she said, going into the kitchen and mixing my drink. When she returned, she added, "I will have one later, when I'm alone." I was not surprised by her reluctance to join me. It would infer equality.

"You've been feisty all your life, Mister Strutwick, and that's gonna hold you in good stead during this trouble."

"Now that you've placed me at the head of the table and fortified me with good bourbon, tell me how my father died." I spoke calmly.

"Oh, dear God in heaven. I hate to say it." She looked away.

"Say it quickly then. I'm relying on your strength," I ordered quietly.

She stared at an oil painting over the Queen Anne sideboard and started. "Mister Hall shot himself at the bank...in his office! Blew his brains out! Trouble over the money coming up short, they told us. Miss Carolyn...she's been almost out of her head, calling and calling here. Then coming over herself with her youngest, little Keith, and leaving him with us."

"The boy's here? But why?"

"Miss Carolyn and Mister Owen been going 'round and 'round, hollering and cursing! Mister Owen is furious, says he's too mortified to go back to work at your daddy's bank. Called him an embezzler! Miss Carolyn brought us Keith 'cause he was fussing with his father. The boy was taking up for our family, and Mister Owen slapped him hard! The child's face's still got a big red place on it!"

"That sonofabitch! I'll see him tomorrow. Who's with Keith?"

"Oh, Mister Strutwick, the child's happy and peaceful now. He settled down when I told him he could sleep in *your* room tonight... 'Just for tonight,' I said." There was a hint of a weak smile around the corners of Mrs. O'Brian's mouth. "He worships the ground you walk on, Mister Strutwick. Always has."

"You did the right thing." I took a deep breath and exhaled slowly. "Well, so much for Oliver Hall. I don't think I'll miss him. And Claire? How is she taking all this?"

I went to the kitchen, still talking to Mrs. O'Brian who followed me. I replenished my drink and noticed that the kitchen was as immaculate as always. This stout housekeeper was a wonder, keeping order during this turmoil.

"It's Miss Claire I don't understand. No, sir, not at all. Calm as she can be. She talked to Miss Carolyn no more than five minutes before sending her home." She grew pensive.

"I was taking Miss Claire some coffee in the family living room when Miss Carolyn came bursting in with the boy. Miss Claire said she would not listen to all that raving, said it was unbecoming a Virginia lady. The child ran over to her chair and threw his arms around her. She fretted over him and had him quieted down like you wouldn't believe!"

"Claire did that?" I had made my second drink much stronger, and it had its relaxing effects. Claire had never seemed a soothing personality.

"She sent Miss Carolyn home to get ahold of herself, said we'd all discuss the situation tomorrow with you. Said you would know the best course to take. Then she went up to her room."

"Umm. There it is," I murmured.

"What's that, Mister Strutwick?"

"Strut takes the reins!" I proclaimed sarcastically.

"Why, for sure you do! Think anybody else 'round here could take charge of the Widdicombe family?"

"I'll do what I can, Mrs. O'Brian, but I'll need your help."

"You've got that," she promised, before going to a cupboard and retrieving an envelope. Offering it to me, she said, "Here's one more thing, Mister Strutwick."

"A letter for me?" I puzzled, taking the envelope and returning to the family dining room, drink in hand. "Is it from my father?" I sat down again at the head of the table.

"It's from Mister Hall, all right, but it's not *to* you. Think you oughta open it, though." She stood beside me.

"It's addressed to a Mrs. Kitty Wenzel in the Selden Apartments. I don't know the woman."

"It was on your father's desk at the bank, so they brought it here. And that's not all. That woman has been calling here since late this afternoon. Keeps asking to speak to Miss Claire."

"Did you let her?" I frowned.

"No, Mister Strut, I sure didn't. Told her she'd have to talk to you." Mrs. O'Brian wrung her hands and looked at me imploringly. "Did I do right?"

"I'll read the letter and then answer your question. You surely did no wrong."

I tore open the envelope and read the letter. It was a farewell note from my father to Kitty Wenzell. He had been in love with her. From the letter I surmised that he had been keeping her for some time. I hated Oliver Hall for this. Claire must not be told; she would be devastated.

"You did the right thing, Mrs. O'Brian. Is this letter all that was brought to the house by the bank's representatives?"

"There are two boxes in the library. Personal effects, they said."

"I will go through those tomorrow. Of course, you did not mention this letter to Mrs. Wenzel when she called?"

"Of course not, Mister Strutwick. She don't know about the letter."

"Then it is a confidence between you and me."

"And the bank people."

"*They* won't be a problem. Now I'm going upstairs to speak to Claire...if she's awake."

"Oh, she's awake. Said she wouldn't go to bed until she talked to you."

I stood up and took Mrs. O'Brian's hand, pressing it between both of mine. "You are a treasure. Don't *worry*. You've managed very well. With time all will be as it should be." Then I released her hand and turned to go.

"But suicide and, and...taking the bank's money...think of the scandal!"

"That was all Oliver Hall's problem," I answered, "and he was not a Widdicombe! We simply have to 'divorce' him...after the fact."

Picking up my luggage, I left the puzzled woman and mounted the rear staircase. Upstairs, I left my bags outside the closed door of my bedroom, so as not to awaken Keith. There was a wedge of light under Claire's door. I knocked.

"Come in, dear." she called. Claire was leaning over her bed, fingering something when I entered. She looked drawn but not distraught. She stopped what she was doing and came toward me.

"Claire, I am here now." I embraced her.

"Strut, I thought you would never come." She smiled and pecked me on the cheek. "There are things to discuss tonight. You'll be so busy tomorrow." She returned to the bed and resumed what she had been doing.

I was thunderstruck. She was not upset, not depressed, and definitely not overly concerned. This was so unlike the Claire I had known, subservient to my father all those years.

Her dark red hair was flowing to her shoulders, instead of pulled back into the familiar severe bun. She was wearing a frilly powder blue wrapper, and she actually looked rather pretty.

"What *are* you doing, Claire?" I asked, going to stand beside her at the bed.

"I am inspecting this French lace, dear. I brought it back from Paris years ago to have it made into a dress and never seemed to get around to it, but now I've decided to. Jessie Cobb told me about a perfectly splendid seamstress on Boush Street, whom I called today...."

"Claire! We have to talk about Father."

"I know." She turned and looked at me. "I hope you are not too terribly sad, Strut. It must be difficult for you."

She left the bedside and seated herself on a Victorian loveseat. I followed and sat in the gentleman's chair next to her.

"I think your sister is having a wretched time of it. You should check on her in the morning. First thing." She folded her hands in her lap and looked at me calmly.

"Certainly. But, Claire, I don't understand you. I expected you to be, umm, well, overwrought, although I'm relieved you are not."

"I am so sorry," she spoke soothingly. "I am not being sensitive. Your father has just shot himself, and I'm running on about French lace."

"Oh, Claire, I'm not suffering! He was *your* husband! As for myself, I don't think I ever loved him."

"Neither did I! Does that surprise you?"

"Well, yes, it does. You've caught me off guard." I smiled sheepishly.

"I *am* sorry he died, and I *am* sorry he embezzled from the bank." Claire rolled her big brown eyes heavenward "But I am released now, free, for the first time in thirty-six years! Oliver was a bit of a tyrant."

"A bit," I said and laughed.

"You shouldn't laugh, Strut...be nice. We must respect the dead. Fetch me some port, please, and have some yourself."

"1 have already had bourbon," I replied, going to the round gate-leg table by the window to pour her wine from a crystal decanter and taking it to her.

"I was only nineteen when I married Oliver," she spoke softly, sipping the port.

"Too young. A year younger than I am now. Grandfather should have kept you in Saint Mary's in Raleigh."

"Yes, younger than you, and not nearly as bright as you, Strut. I believe I married beneath myself, but it was Papa's doing. He arranged it. Oliver and I never did love each other."

"Do you realize that we have related to, communicated with, each other more in these past few minutes than we have in all the years before?" I was discovering that I enjoyed my mother very much.

"And we will have many more family chats, Strut. I feel that our lives will be happier now."

"But there are problems to be faced. I imagine the bank auditors will have to be reckoned with," I said.

'You will need some help with that. I'll call the nice young man at church who is a CPA. He can straighten out the debts and guide you into handling our finances."

"Who is that, Claire?"

"You should remember. His name is Neil Rice. He always stops to greet us after service at Saint Paul's...seems especially interested in you, dear."

"I remember him," I agreed, recalling the man.

Claire was correct in saying Neil Rice was especially interested in me. He usually cornered me in the church vestibule and questioned me about school, or anything he could think of, just to keep me there. I suspected he had a more personal than social interest in me.

"Yes, do call him. Ask him if I can see him tomorrow afternoon."

"There are the funeral arrangements to be made, too," she said. "I want the service to be held at Saint Paul's, not in a funeral parlor."

Of course it would be in our parish church. Claire was staunch Episcopalian; she thought that members of other denominations were, at best, misled Christians. The Widdicombes had been Episcopalian for eons, and before that they had been Church of England.

"Tomorrow I will see to all that," I assured her. "Is Saturday afternoon acceptable to you?"

"That will be fine, Strut, But, oh, I don't want to wear black. I feel older in black."

"Grey should do nicely, After all, this is 1970."

"Tomorrow I'll get a permanent." She emptied her glass. "And I can wear my sable coat for the funeral. Refill my glass, dear."

"We Widdicombes are a curious breed." I grinned when I handed Claire her wine. "Who would have guessed that you would be talking about permanents and sable coats only hours after Oliver died? Even I wouldn't have."

"Yes, we are curious, aren't we?" she said, fixing her eyes on the closed door to Oliver's room. They had had connecting bedrooms.

"Don't become sentimental now, Claire."

"Oh, I'm not. I was thinking about Oliver's bedroom. It could become a lovely sitting room for me. What do you think?" She continued to sip the port.

"Fine, but wait until after the funeral."

She nodded to signify that the matter was settled. Then I thought about my bedroom nearby and the difficulties I would have in slipping Vic upstairs at night. It could be an uncomfortable situation.

"Next week we shall make several changes to accommodate us both," I spoke firmly. "I will move my bedroom downstairs into the family-private living room. The furniture there will be at your disposal for your parlor."

The family living room, the kitchen, and the family dining room, all at the rear of the house, had doors that opened onto the walled garden. My proposed change would make it much easier for Vic and me to have late night trysts.

"Oh. You'd sleep downstairs? I think I understand," she smiled. "But not after you marry."

"Marriage is definitely not in my plans, Claire."

She was silent then, possibly weighing the implication of my words against the prospects of my marriage being a means of replenishing the Widdicombe coffers.

"There are two rooms on the third floor stuffed with family antiques. I shall choose from them to furnish my sitting room."

Contriving to appear relaxed, I stretched and stifled a yawn.

"You are tired, I know, but there is something else, someone else, we have to talk about."

"Yes, I know. Keith is here...in my bedroom asleep. It's all right."

"His father is upset with us, our family—blames us for Oliver's thievery...his suicide, too." Claire swirled the port in its glass. "Being in the same bank with Oliver does make it particularly awkward for Owen."

"As I understand it, Oliver got Owen his position in the bank," I mused.

"Indeed he did. But now Owen Fleming is very embarrassed, and he is raising hell with Carolyn. Keith was defending her, defending all of us actually, when Owen struck him."

"Carolyn was right in bringing Keith to us," I stated. "The boy's always been happy here."

"Keith is so like you were at eleven, Strut. I want to keep him here. Permanently."

"Why, for god's sake?"

"To rear him as a Widdicombe. To give him the love and attention I didn't give you and Carolyn when you were children."

"And to perpetuate the Widdicombe lineage since I won't be impregnating a spouse?"

"Oh, Strut, hush!" Claire smiled. "I'm blushing, I do believe."

"It becomes you. However, I do agree. If it can be arranged, Keith shall stay. He's the pick of the litter."

"Kyle and Kevin do keep Carolyn on her toes."

"I wish Keith had our dark red hair," I commented.

"He probably will, by the time he's grown. It is auburn now, and it will surely darken."

"I must go to bed. I'm tired to the bone, Claire." I stood up. "I don't feel just twenty years old tonight."

"And you never will again."

Claire stood also, and our eyes met. Her words had been totally honest and accurate. I would never feel twenty again. We walked toward the door together.

"Pity poor Kitty Wenzel. She must be grieving terribly," she murmured.

I gasped and turned to her. "You know?" I exclaimed. "You know about father and Kitty Wenzel?"

"Why, yes, for years. Everyone in Norfolk knows. I did what I could to encourage their affair. But Oliver did not know that I knew. I simply made it easy for him to see her."

"Why didn't you care?"

"Everyone needs to be loved, Strut, and that should include Oliver, too."

"I...believe we *are* a curious breed, Claire!"

She smiled and gave me a light kiss on the cheek as I opened the door. "I have a penchant for oysters. Do tell Mrs. O'Brian in the morning to have them at dinner. Fried, I believe, dear."

I agreed and then left her. Opening my door, I slipped the luggage in quietly. I did not want to wake Keith. Mrs. O'Brian had left a small lamp on for me. Not attempting to unpack my bags, I stripped to my undershorts and turned out the light. I eased into bed beside the still form and thought how marvelous the bed felt.

"Why didn't you put on your pajamas, Strut?" Keith's gentle voice whispered.

The voice startled me, and I made a sudden involuntary movement. "What's the matter?" he asked softly.

"I thought you were asleep, Kei, and I didn't want to fumble around and wake you. Furthermore, I'm too tired to care about pajamas."

"Oh," he murmured.

"Sorry I woke you. Let's go to sleep now."

"Sure. I'm glad you're back from Lexington, Strut," he said and leaned over. He kissed me on the ear, missing my cheek in the dark.

"Goodnight, Kei. We will talk at breakfast."

"Kei... I like that. K E I. The I makes the E say its name."

I knew then that I loved the boy and fell asleep with a smile on my face.

CHAPTER TWO

When I sat down to breakfast in the family dining room, I had already talked to the funeral home's representative, as well as our priest at Saint Paul's. The service and interment were scheduled for Saturday afternoon.

"It's to be at two o'clock Saturday," I informed Claire, unfolding my linen napkin.

"Are you sad, Strut?" Keith, who was sitting next to me, asked.

"No, I am not, Kei," I smiled at him and patted his shoulder. "We have to accept the way things are and then restore order in our lives."

"Did grandfather really shoot himself because he took money from his bank?"

"Yes, he did," Claire interposed. She was seated opposite me at the far end of the table.

"That's why my dad's so mad. He said it ruined our family name. And Kyle and Kevin are on his side. They believe it, too."

Mrs. O'Brian came in with a silver coffee pot and filled our cups. "Not much in mine, Mrs. O'Brian. I want to add a lot of cream to it," Keith smiled at her.

"I know, half and half. Nobody knows better'n me how you like your coffee," she answered brightly.

"Well, I told them it was a pack of lies," Keith declared, looking from Claire to me. "Was I wrong?"

"Not altogether, Keith," Claire answered. "Our family name is not ruined. We are Widdicombes, and your grandfather was not."

"If there is a stain on our family name," I told the boy, "then we shall have to erase it."

"Oh," Keith looked puzzled. "I don't think I understand, Strut."

"You will, Kei," I answered him. "It will take time, but understanding will come."

"Sure," he grinned at me, "if I'm stained a little, I don't care. I just like to hear you talk. You sound like a Duke or something,"

We all laughed and looked at the food Mrs. O'Brian was putting down before us.

"Super!" Keith declared, as he began serving himself a mound of sausage patties. "Best in town," he complimented her.

"Have eggs and biscuits, too, dear," Claire insisted.

"I wish I could stay here forever," Keith declared between mouthfuls.

I was finishing when Mrs. O'Brian called me to the phone. It was Owen Fleming, my humiliated brother-in-law. I left Claire and Kei, picking up the phone in the library.

"Strutwick, thank god you are finally home!" he began. "At last I can talk to someone in this family who makes sense!"

"Yes, Owen, I do make sense, and I am interested in hearing all you have to say. I am especially interested in knowing why you slapped your eleven-year-old son!"

"What the hell? I don't have to answer to you! He's my son!"

"Perhaps you prefer to answer to the courts. Claire knows a judge who can advise us. I believe they grew up together!" I bluffed.

"I can discipline my own son—"

"Slapping isn't disciplining, Owen. Both Claire and Mrs. O'Brian saw your fingermarks on his face yesterday! Should I make the call?"

"You F.F.V.'s think you've got the world by the tail, don't you?"

"What does F.F.V. mean, Owen?"

"You know goddamn well that it means First Families of Virginia! The high and mighty Widdicombe family thinks it invented the Commonwealth!"

"Thank you. I had thought for a moment that the initials stood for something obscene!"

Although I could hear Carolyn crying in the background, I was determined to stay on the offensive with this insecure social climber.

"You're in for one hell of a scandal, young man! And I'm not staying around to be dragged down with you people."

"Your true colors are showing, Owen. Let me remind you that the Widdicombes did not embezzle, and the Widdicombes did not put any bullets through their heads! Oliver Hall did, and he only married into the family. The truth is, the Widdicombes have sometimes made unsatisfactory choices in spouses."

"Huh?"

"I am saying you actually have nothing to fear, Owen."

"If you think I'm staying here, you are out of your mind! I'm leaving Carolyn, and I'm taking the boys with me! They have been hurt enough."

"Not Keith! You aren't taking Keith anywhere!"

"Oh, no? And why not?"

"Keith is loyal, not only to Carolyn, but to Claire and myself. Do you wish to hear it from the boy's own lips, Owen? Now settle down, and, if you are capable of thinking rationally, we can probably come to an agreement, You told me you are leaving Carolyn. Are you thinking divorce?" I had been thinking along these lines as we talked.

"Definitely. Carolyn knows that. The bank understands my predicament, and they're transferring me to the Roanoke branch." Owen was sullen. "I intend to raise my boys in new surroundings."

"Claire and I can convince Carolyn not to seek alimony or custody of Kyle and Kevin, but we would have to have legal custody of Keith. Will you sign papers to that effect?" It was the first solution to come into my head, but I thought it was worth trying.

"Legal custody of Keith? To Carolyn? She's too damn scatter-brained!"

"Then custody to Claire?"

"Hell, he's probably one of *your* kind, anyway."

I let the remark pass. Too much was at risk.

"Carolyn could sign a binding agreement at the same time," I persisted, "stating she would seek neither alimony nor custody of Kyle or Kevin. If you and Carolyn go through court proceedings, she might get custody of all three." I was filling in the gaps as I went along.

Owen reluctantly agreed, and the rest of the morning was organized confusion. Claire drove over and persuaded Carolyn, who was hardly coherent, to do as I had proposed. Claire wanted Keith at all costs. In addition she was glad to break with a son-in-law she had never liked.

I called the family lawyer and set up a one o'clock appointment. When we arrived, we found that Owen had brought Kyle and Kevin with him. They made it clear that they preferred to live with their father. I had Mrs. O'Brian keep Keith in an anteroom until he was needed to state his wishes. Carolyn did little more than weep, but she, as well as Owen, assigned full legal custody of Keith to Claire. It couldn't be that easy, I thought to myself.

After all the documents had been signed, everyone stood up to leave. Claire, with custody of Keith tucked away in her purse, said something about killing two birds with one shot. That silenced everybody, even me. I was trying not to laugh.

I was driving Oliver's Mercedes Benz with Keith seated beside me. Claire, Carolyn, and Mrs. O'Brian were in the back seat. Stopping at the mortuary, I went in alone and selected the coffin. I left clothes for Oliver that Mrs. O'Brian had gotten together earlier.

Once we were home, Carolyn went to her bedroom to lie down, and Claire closed herself up in the library to use the phone. One of the maids told me that Kitty Wenzel had called me twice.

"What do you think of all this legal maneuvering, Kei?" I asked the boy.

"I don't understand most of it, Strut, but if it means I can stay here with you, then I'm all for it."

"That is exactly the part I like best, too, Kei."

"I want Mother to feel better, though. She cries a lot."

"Your mother has lost a lot. You see, even though your father doesn't love her anymore, she still loves him."

"I don't think I do, Strut. Love Dad, I mean. He loves Kyle and Kevin, but not me. He calls me a sissy."

"I've been called a sissy, too. Learn to ignore such remarks, Kei."

"Sure, okay. And Kyle and Kevin. I won't miss them at all. Kevin used to beat me up, and Kyle wouldn't stop him...just watch."

"You have another home now." I tousled his auburn hair. "And it does not include your brothers. They will not be received here."

"Super!" Keith threw his arms around my waist and hugged me. I laughed and, reaching down, hugged back.

"Think perhaps you could go up to your mother's room and try to make her feel better?"

I could see Claire in the doorway to the library. She was beckoning to me.

"Yes. When she knows how happy I am, maybe she'll be happy, too."

"Try."

"I'll try hard," he said, as he bounded up the curved staircase. I went to Claire, and, taking me by the hand, she ushered me into the library and slid the doors closed.

"Keith is delighted, isn't he?"

"Yes, and, Claire, I am, too. I love the boy. We did do the right thing."

"Yes, we did. Now we need to snap Carolyn out of her mourning. She has taken to her bed."

"It will take time," I advised. "She was in a no-win situation."

"She needs to regain her self-confidence. I'll go up and talk to her. But what I wanted to tell you is that I phoned Neil Rice."

"Oh?"

"And he is on his way over. You two close yourselves up in here and go through our financial situation. I don't know a thing about money."

"Except how to spend it."

"Oh, yes, I do know that," she smiled, "but otherwise, money is vulgar. Oliver kept the bills in the desk, so it's in your hands."

"That I realize."

"But the deed to the house. I have that in the wall safe in my bedroom. I'll send it down by Keith."

"Is Oliver's name on the deed, Claire?"

"Oh, no, just my name, although we should include your name now."

"Next week. We shall have it changed next week," I told her.

"I'm leaving in an hour to have my hair done," she told me. Then she left me alone in the library.

While waiting for the CPA, I called Kitty Wenzel. She referred to herself as a "friend" of my father and profusely expressed her shock and sorrow, declaring a great need to talk to me in person. I promised her I would call at her apartment after dinner.

When Neil Rice arrived, a maid showed him into the library and then slid the doors shut, He was younger than I had remembered. I stepped forward and shook his hand.

"Welcome, Mister Rice. I appreciate your coming."

"It's a privilege, Strutwick," he smiled. "I've known you and your family for years, and I'll help any way I can."

He extended his regrets in the loss of my father and asked to be called by his first name, telling me he was only twenty-eight. In return I expressed my preference for Strut, rather than Strutwick. I felt comfortable in his company.

"The entire management of the family is passing into my hands, Neil, and I am very much the novice in financial matters. Assume I know nothing about this—I am your willing student."

"You have a certain, almost formal manner of speaking—" Neil looked at me tentatively as he removed his coat.

"Yes, it reinforces my sense of individuality," I smiled sincerely at him.

"What's your college major, Strut?" he asked.

"English," I answered, and we both laughed.

Sitting side by side behind the large desk, both of us went through every drawer, as well as the boxes sent over by the bank, studying policies and itemizing debts. I was dismayed to learn that Oliver had taken out such a small amount of life insurance on himself. Moreover, the total indebtedness was high. Some bills were past due. Neil took off his tie and rolled up his sleeves. The man worked for hours on the figures.

"There isn't a lot of money in his checking account," Neil said, leaning back in his chair and looking worried, "and you can't touch that right now. It goes into the estate."

"I don't know how I'll pay these bills or feed my family," I said tightly.

"I can loan you a thousand, Strut. It could help tide you over until you secure employment."

Neil took off his glasses and put them in his pocket. He looked at me sympathetically. His brown hair was mussed, tumbling onto his forehead. I realized then that he was nice looking. At church he had always been dressed so properly. Now, with his shirt sleeves rolled up and his glasses off, he had a certain charm. I could also appreciate the fact that he was more masculine than I remembered.

"I don't want to take unfair advantage of our friendship, Neil." I tried to appraise his interest in me. It had been evident at church on a number of occasions. I put my hand on his lower arm, resting it there.

His brown eyes brightened, and, smiling, he insisted, "It's something I want to do."

Thanking him, I gave him a peck on the cheek before I stood up and moved away, going to stand by a window. My back was to Neil and I stared at the street outside. The sky had become bleak because a cold front was moving in. A chill coursed through my body. Even though I presented a commanding demeanor to the world, I felt immature and afraid. Only twenty and without experience, I knew nothing about earning an income, an income sufficient to provide for my family.

"What should I do first?" I said, turning to face Neil.

"Cut expenses drastically," he answered. "I'll go to the bank to check on the extent of your family's liability...in the embezzlement."

"Then I should call the bank, let them know you are our representative."

Neil stood up, his eyes searching my face. I think he was trying to gauge how personal my interest in him was.

"Yes, call today, and I'll be there when it opens tomorrow."

"Neil, we'll go under if we're liable," I spoke quietly.

"You could sell the house if you have to."

"If I did that, it would be the end of the Widdicombes."

"The Widdicombes *are* Norfolk," Neil reflected, shaking his head. "Since 1736."

I held his coat for him to slip into, and then he was gone. We needed his thousand just to make it through Christmas, I realized. Then I wondered what type of employment I could find. Returning to Lexington was definitely out of the question.

By dinnertime I had taken the first steps to economize. Dismissing our two maids with regrets, I paid their earned wages from money I still had in pocket for college expenses. My thoughts next centered on our three cars: Oliver's Mercedes, Claire's Cadillac, and my Jaguar. Two of them would have to be sold. Neil had discovered that money was still owing on the Cadillac and the Jaguar, so I decided to keep the Mercedes. I called dealers about Claire's and my cars and was told to bring them in tomorrow.

Tomorrow was Friday. Vic would have his last exam in the morning and then would drive to Norfolk. He should be here before dinner. I needed him, needed his support. He had always maintained that I was the stronger one, but my stamina was almost depleted. Just to see Vic would help me to cope.

At dinner Claire questioned me about my dismissing the maids, but I insisted that we not discuss it until after we ate. She enjoyed her fried oysters and waited.

When we finished, we moved to the family living room, and I asked Mrs. O'Brian and Keith to be present, too. I explained how poor our financial condition was and informed them that I could not return to Washington and Lee. Then I gave my attention to Mrs. O'Brian.

"Without you in this house my life won't be the same. Frankly, I cannot even imagine it, but we have no choice. There simply is no money to pay your wages."

Claire gasped, and Keith's face crumpled.

"Mister Strutwick, I'm as much a part of this family as the rest of you...in my own way," Mrs. O'Brian began. "There's gonna be hard times, but I'm staying. I won't walk out when you need me the most. My room up on the third floor suits me just fine, and I'll work for nothing 'til you see you're able to pay me again. Besides, I can do delicious things with rice."

"My god, you are a saint!" I exclaimed, jumping up and hugging her. "I love you, and I'll not give you a chance to change your mind!"

"There's a little money I've got put away. It's yours when you need it." Mrs. O'Brian began retreating from the room.

"Not on your life," I sailed after her. "That is exactly where we draw the line!"

"You can always change your mind, but I've got two trays for upstairs tonight, so excuse me. Food don't stay hot forever." Then she was gone.

"Two trays?" Keith asked, looking at Claire and me. "Who else, besides Mother?"

"Never mind, Keith," Claire directed. "It's something we cannot discuss with you until you are older."

"Tomorrow I'm going to go all over this house, from top to bottom! It's my home, too," Keith announced.

"You are not!" I spoke up.

"But that's not fair!"

"It is my unpleasant duty to tell you that the world is not fair, Kei," I informed him.

"Old families have strange secrets, Keith." Claire tried to pacify the boy.

"Are there any maids living on the third floor?" he persisted.

"Mrs. O'Brian is our only live-in servant, and she's more than a servant," Claire answered. "Why, I was only fifteen when she came to us."

"And you are not to plague her with questions, Kei." I was unyielding.

"Okay, but some day, when I'm older, you have to tell—"

"I promise, Kei," I interrupted.

"Tomorrow, after we bring your clothes and things over," Claire diverted the boy's attention, "we'll move you into your own room."

"Yes, and I will be moving my bedroom downstairs, in here, in fact...in a few days."

"Then I'll stay put," Keith decided. I like your bedroom, Strut, and its got a bathroom."

Claire and I looked at each other. Why not? We hadn't put it into words in our conversations, but Claire and I understood that we intended to groom Keith to become the master of Widdicombe House eventually. 'Why not begin his residency by giving him a bedroom that had its own private bathroom? There were only two such bedrooms on the second floor, Claire's and mine. She nodded her head.

"If you want my room, you shall have it," I said, and the youngster was content.

My grandfather, Cedric Widdicombe, had improved the entire plumbing scheme of the house. Because of him we could situate Keith in a room with private bath. Prior to the patriarch's efforts the house had had only two bathrooms, one on the second floor and the other on the third floor. Not only had my grandfather added the half-bath downstairs, he had installed private bathrooms in the rooms that were now Claire's and mine, as well as in Aunt Charlotte's room on the third floor. At age eleven, Keith was expressing his desire for privacy, and we could accommodate him.

Imagining Keith exploring, as he had threatened to do, caused me to mentally survey the house and grounds. Our home certainly wasn't the largest in Norfolk, but it was one of the oldest, and it was the only one of the very old homes in which one family had continuously resided. Each generation had made alterations and improvements, but the house retained its regal charm, the flavor of a time long since passed.

Built in 1887, it was situated on old Freemason Street which was referred to as cobblestoned. Actually the street was made of bricks; it had never experienced modern paving.

The Widdicombe House was Victorian, constructed of red brick, and its small front yard was bordered with the original black iron fence. Adjacent to the house was a carriage house, now used for automobiles. In the rear was a brick walled garden, with Cape jasmine shrubs, two magnolia trees, and Claire's rose garden. A wooden gazebo, painted white and with seats inside, stood in the center.

Entering through the leaded-glass front door of the house, newcomers were impressed with the high ceilings and tall windows. The entrance hall or vestibule was oak-paneled from floor to ceiling. Sliding doors opened into the drawing room, library, music room, and formal dining room. On the landing of the curved staircase was a window seat under a bay window, also of leaded glass.

Across the rear of the first floor were the family dining room, the family living room (soon to be my bedroom), and the kitchen with walk-in pantry and a dumb waiter that was used to hoist food trays to the upper floors. The powder room was under the front staircase.

On the second floor were Claire's and Oliver's connecting bedrooms and her private bathroom, my bedroom (soon to be Keith's) with private bathroom, Carolyn's bedroom, two guest bedrooms, and the hall bathroom.

The third floor had originally been intended for servants' quarters only. It now had Aunt Charlotte's room with connecting bathroom, Mrs. O'Brian's room, an unused servant's room, two rooms used to store family furniture, and the hall bathroom.

Both Claire and I had known no other home, and we emotionally embraced the house. It was a pivotal component of our lives, and it was my task to keep all of us in it.

My mind had strayed, and I forced my attention back to Claire and Keith. Someday the boy would love Widdicombe House as much as I did.

"Perhaps tomorrow morning you could drive over to Owen's,"

I said, refocusing my attention on our present situation, "and pick up Keith's things, Claire."

"And Carolyn's, too," she responded.

"Speaking of driving, I have to go over to the Selden Apartments," I remembered.

"Oh? To see Jessie Cobb?"

"No, Claire. Another resident...Mrs. Wenzel. She has requested my presence."

"My, my, poor Kitty 'Wenzel. Tell her, dear, to attend the funeral, if she wishes. I don't mind at all."

An elderly doorman with silver hair admitted me to the lobby of the Selden Apartments. While he called Mrs. Wenzel for permission to send me up, I looked around the lobby. This was no modern structure of chrome and glass. The building probably had the distinction of being Norfolk's first high-rise apartment house. The lobby was furnished with Victorian sofas and chairs, and on its old tile floor were two large oriental rugs. Ferns stood in large stands in corners.

Hanging up the phone, the doorman nodded for me to go up. As I ascended to the sixth floor in the highly-polished brass elevator cage, I decided the ride was as smooth as those I had had in the more modern lifts.

Upstairs I stood on thick patterned carpet and rang the doorbell. Kitty Wenzel opened the door and ushered me inside. She was tall and too thin, with piercing dark eyes and a strong chin. She was a brunette; her hair was wavy and cut rather short. Her dress was of black satin and adorned with black lace at the throat. She did not strike me as ever having been an attractive woman, which surprised me.

"So you are Oliver's son," she spoke quietly. "Sit down, please."

I murmured something polite and sat on her sofa. The furniture was contemporary, and the room was decorated in subdued colors. Neither the apartment nor Mrs. Wenzel were what I had expected. I think I had imagined it would be gaudy and over-decorated, as the homes of mistresses were so often depicted in the cinema.

"Your name is Strutwick, isn't it? Call me Kitty. No need for formalities." Her voice was calm and friendly, but her eyes were hard, and her mouth a thin tight line. "Such a shock, Oliver's suicide. Gone without even a goodbye." She sat down beside me on the sofa. "I'll miss him so much."

"It is a difficult time for the family, too," I said.

"The family! Your family didn't love him the way I did!" she suddenly flared.

"I see." I stiffened but remained noncommittal.

"He was the world to me! We were in love! Your mother doesn't know that. We were discreet about our relationship."

"You have suffered a serious loss. I realize that, Mrs. Wenzel." I was uncomfortable.

She stood up and went to a table, took up a cigarette from a crystal box and lit it.

"Even though Oliver was somewhat older than I, I loved him...and he loved me. He was my world!" She dabbed at her dry eyes with a handkerchief. "I'll be lost without him. Utterly lost!"

"His death is a tragedy that we all have to accept," I began. "But it has happened, and that is that. We must accept it and go on."

"Go on? How? He was planning to buy a house for me, of my own—take me out of this apartment!"

"I don't have the answers for you, Mrs. Wenzel. I'm still seeking answers for us."

"Your family has plenty. You could easily purchase a house for me. You'd never miss the money."

"I? You mean you wish me to buy you a home?"

"Yes. I'll live quietly, not causing any scandal for the Widdicombes. I only want what Oliver promised me!"

"My mother and I made no promise!" I was angry. "As for scandal, the entire city knows about you and Oliver! That damage was done years ago!"

"You don't understand!" She half shouted at me. "I don't have anything! Oliver always took care of all my expenses. This isn't fair!"

I stood up and walked over to her, understanding now why she had sent for me. Even if we had the money, I wouldn't spend any of it on her.

"I don't *care* whether Oliver had an affair with you or not, but you'll not see a dime of Widdicombe money! Excuse me, I'll leave now!"

I turned toward the door, but Kitty Wenzel thrust herself against it, blocking the way.

"You're effeminate, aren't you?" Her smile was twisted, cruel. "Oliver said you were probably a homosexual. Suppose *that* gets around Norfolk!"

My silent rage increased, feeding on itself.

"Why, no bank in town would hire you!" she continued. "You'd be shunned! And I do know many of Oliver's associates rather well! A word from me and—"

"I have never been closeted about my sexual preference, dear Mrs. 'Wenzel! I don't give a happy damn who knows I'm gay! You are an opportunist, and not a very clever one at that. Furthermore, it has been the Widdicombe in-laws in banking, not the Widdicombes themselves. Now move away from that door!"

She leaned her head back and against the door. Smiling, she reached out and touched the lapel of my coat. Her expression softened suspiciously.

"I'm overwrought and saying things I don't mean, Strutwick." She caressed the fabric of my coat. "Why don't we sit down and have a cocktail?"

With one sudden movement I reached out, shoving her away from the door with one hand and flinging it open with the other.

"See you at the funeral, bitch!" I spat, and then I was gone. Waiting for the elevator, I heard Kitty Wenzel slam her door.

When I reached home, I was still seething over the audacity of Kitty Wenzel. What she had attempted was obvious blackmail. Not fit to make polite conversation with Claire, I closed myself up in the library. She had already designated it as my work space, my office.

Looking at the hundreds of books on the built-in bookshelves that reached the ceiling, I decided to read something that would calm me before going to bed. I walked over to a shelf and scanned titles at eye level. Nothing appealed to me.

Then I remembered that last summer, Oliver had suggested I spend time reading the Widdicombe journals. Actually they were a compilation of handwritten and typed pages, letters, notes, and family trees, all in chronological order and bound together. At the time I hadn't the inclination to read them because I was caught up in partying and yachting with Vic. But now the journals assumed more importance to me. Last summer I was a college boy, looking for fun and excitement, but tonight I was the master of Widdicombe House, depended upon to solve all its problems.

Opening a cabinet under the shelves, I removed the journals and then settled with them in a Queen Anne wing chair beside a good light. I decided not to tackle all of it at once but to leaf through, reading a few sections that captured my interest.

Our earliest American ancestor was John Widdicombe. As a young Englishman he had been the protégé of an Alexander Campbell who was one of Norfolk's first aldermen. In 1736 Campbell had financed John in his building of two warehouses for the storage of tobacco and food items to be shipped through this colonial port to England. Maybe old John Widdicombe's English forebears had not been very distinguished. There was no mention of them at all.

Scanning pages rapidly, I realized that I was becoming sleepy. I was about to put the journals away when I noticed an important entry.

With this one occurrence, the Widdicombes had lost many of the clan. The Yellow Fever Plague of 1855, brought to Norfolk by a steamer bound for New York, wiped out more than two thousand of the city's citizens, including all but one branch, our branch, of course, of the Widdicombe family. The one surviving branch had closed its house and fled the city by carriage. They took refuge in Durham, North Carolina, until it was safe to return to Norfolk.

This entry perked my interest, and the memory of Kitty Wenzel was dispelled. I felt pride in the spirit of that 1855 Widdicombe family. Smiling sleepily, I stashed away the journals. I wasn't the first of the family to face possible disaster or ruin. Now, as then, the Widdicombes would confront their problems and cope. We don't surrender; we are survivors!

CHAPTER THREE

"Get up, Strut," said Kei, shaking my shoulder. He was already dressed and smiling over me. "Claire says to hurry on downstairs, that there's lots to do."

"Perhaps ten minutes longer." I yawned and closed my eyes again.

"No, now!" he insisted, and he pulled the covers off me.

I got out of bed and stretched before I went to the bathroom to throw cold water on my face. When I returned, Kei was making up the bed. "Are you on maid duty today?" I smiled at the boy. "Claire told me to make the beds."

He stopped and watched me dress. It was evident that he was interested in my anatomy, so I turned my back until I was into my trousers.

"You are referring to your grandmother by her given name?"

"She told me to, and I told her to call me Kei. That's what I want to be called from now on...by everybody."

"'Tis a new life for us all," I remarked.

Leaving Kei to finish his chores, I ambled downstairs, thinking black coffee, and heard Claire on the phone through the open door to the family living room. I went in and waited, should she need me.

"Owen, there's no other 'good' time until after the funeral. We've so much to do here...Don't be difficult...Just take the boys out for breakfast! I shall be there within the hour."

I chuckled. Claire was dealing with Owen very well. The butterfly had fully emerged from its cocoon.

"Strut, if I retrieve nothing from that damn house," she said to me after hanging up, "but Carolyn's ruby choker and earrings, I'll be content."

"They belonged to your grandmother, didn't they?"

"They certainly did, and she was a Strutwick."

"Ah, my namesake great-grandmother. Bring the jewelry back if you have to steal!"

"Should I pick you up somewhere? By the time you finish your tasks, you'll be without transportation."

"Oh, no. I'll be just fine. But do remember to stop by your car dealer before going to Owen's. The papers should be ready and waiting for your signature."

As soon as Kei came down, we ate breakfast and then dispersed. Claire, Kei, and Mrs. O'Brian went to Owen's house to retrieve Carolyn's and Kei's clothes and belongings. One at a time I carried my Jaguar and Claire's Cadillac to their respective dealers and sold the cars back to them. It was a long and tiresome process, but, although Oliver had been making the payments on the automobiles, he had purchased them in Claire's and my names.

Once that was completed, a car salesman drove me downtown, and I dropped in on Neil Rice at his office. It was a one-man operation, and the office space was small.

He beamed at me when I came through the door. After we greeted each other, I pulled a chair up close to his and sat down.

"There's some good news from the bank," Neil began.

"I'm ready for good news."

"Oliver Hall was blanket-bonded, or something like that. It seems all the bank employees are, even vice presidents."

"Praise god!" I exclaimed.

"But the loss is not trivial, Strut. There's over two hundred thousand dollars not accounted for. Your father's been, er, busy."

"Where did it all go?" I wondered aloud. "Kitty Wenzel didn't get it. Or, at least I don't believe she did."

"You know about her?" Neil was surprised.

"Yes, and Claire has known all along. I went to see Mrs. Wenzel last night. She summoned me."

"This is beyond belief!"

"'Tis a modern world we live in, Neil. But the point I want to make is that I do not believe she received any large amount of money from Oliver because she gave me the impression she was left high and dry."

"Could she have been lying to you?"

"She could, but I don't think so. She wanted me, or Claire and me, to buy a house for her. She said Oliver had promised her a house."

"That remark had to fall on deaf ears!"
"But she was intimidating."
"How do you mean?"
"She implied that she had connections and could hinder my securing desirable employment in Norfolk. She also made an attempt to use my sexuality to get a house out of us."
"I don't understand."
"The woman said she'd spread the word that I am homosexual." I looked into Neil's eyes as I spoke. "She did not have an answer when I replied that I had never tried to hide that fact."
Neil blushed and looked down at his desk. After a few moments he broke the silence.
"Mrs. Wenzel thought she could steam roll over a twenty year-old boy." He looked into my eyes and continued. "Kitty Wenzel met her match in you, Strut."
"She may do some damage, but I have to risk that. In the end I lost my temper and called her a bitch."
Neil laughed and clasped me around the neck. I knew he was proud of me.
"Let me write you that check while it's on my mind."
Taking out his checkbook, Neil readjusted his sitting posture and wrote. As he did, his leg edged closer and pressed against mine. I did not pull away.
"Visitation is tonight, isn't it?" he said, handing me the check.
"From seven until nine."
I slowly moved my leg up and down against his. It flustered him, but he tried to remain calm.
"I'll be there. Is there anything I can do to help?"
"You just have, Neil," I answered, waving his check in the air. "I appreciate your concern...very much."
I smiled at him as we shook hands, and then I left. Neil seemed to be very much into shaking hands. Maybe it was his way of showing me he liked me. I preferred a peck on the cheek, myself. Even Vic wouldn't object to that. Neil was helping me, and I was grateful.
Stopping in the bank that was the primary rival of Oliver's "money tree," I opened a checking account by depositing Neil's and the car checks. These funds would support us into 1971 if we were

frugal.

I decided to give the city transit system my business and caught a bus. It proved to be convenient, coming within two blocks of Widdicombe House.

When I walked in the front door, I was thinking of Vic, wondering what time he would get in town. It was eleven forty-five, according to the grandfather clock in the vestibule. Vic should have finished his last examination. In an hour or so he would be driving toward Norfolk. I was anxious to see him, hungry for his strong embrace.

I heard someone vacuuming in the drawing room, and, looking through the open doors, I saw that it was Claire, with some sort of cloth over her hair. Happily surprised, I went in and kissed her cheek. She turned off the machine and smiled.

"We're putting the downstairs in order for tonight, dear. Kei is feather-dusting the music room, and Mrs. O'Brian is preparing chicken sandwiches and hot tea for our little lunch."

"Does Kei have a rag on his head, too?" I teased.

"Oh, Strut!" Claire put a hand to the cloth over her hair. "My hair was just done yesterday!"

"I know, I know," I beamed at her, "and everything will look lovely tonight. I'm proud of you...and Kei."

"But don't be disappointed if we have very few callers. I think we are pariahs to this 'Johnny-come-lately' society of today."

"And do we care?"

"Not at all. I think I *would* care if they flooded the house tonight. But Jessie will be here, and she's the one that matters. Vic will come, too, I'm sure."

"I'll welcome his support," I responded.

"Take a few moments and go talk to your sister, dear. Try to get her downstairs for luncheon with us."

Upstairs I found Carolyn, still in her silk negligee, lying in bed and staring at the ceiling.

"I came to convince you to come down to luncheon, Carolyn," I said, sitting in an English armchair beside her. "It would be pleasant to have your company."

"No. I have a headache. I've had it for days."

"Don't you think it's tension-induced? These past days have been difficult."

"Keep Keith out of my room! The child makes my head worse. I don't feel up to listening to him."

"Your son loves you, Carolyn. He's trying to comfort you."

"He can help by leaving me alone. Thank god Kyle and Kevin aren't here, too. Three little monsters would drive me out of my mind. I'm not well, Strut. I need to see a doctor."

"Is the first of the week satisfactory with you? Once the funeral is behind us, I promise I will do all I can for you."

"Father's funeral!" Carolyn rose to a sitting position on the edge of the bed and stared at me. Her eyes had a wild look. "I can't believe he's dead! I won't accept this story about his shooting himself. There must be more to it than they're telling me."

"Try not to dwell on it now. Time for all that later." I patted her hand, and she jerked it behind her. "I will assist you in putting your clothes away, if you'd like."

"Don't touch them! Leave them in the suitcases! I don't want to unpack. Owen will be coming for me, once he's come to his senses!"

This was a very unrealistic statement, but I did not contradict her. She wasn't weeping, as she had been, although it was clear that she did not have a strong grasp on reality. As I looked at her, her face went vacant, expressionless. Unless there was a major change, I would be sure that she saw her doctor Monday.

"Perhaps so," I consoled her. Then I slipped out.

After lunch on the wing, Claire, Mrs. O'Brian, and Kei resumed their cleaning chores, and from the library I phoned the dean of men at Washington and Lee. Informing him that I was definitely withdrawing from college, I requested that he have my clothes packed and shipped to me. There was a light knock on the doors of the library, and Claire came in.

"About through cleaning?" I asked.

"Almost. Little Kei is working his fingers to the bone. I'm proud of the boy."

"Carolyn doesn't want him in her room. Claims he makes her headaches worse."

"Oh." Claire looked grim. "And he's been such an angel to her."

"You are taking over in the mothering department well, Claire.

Kei will do fine."

"Yes, he will, but, actually, I came in to ask you what Neil Rice found out at the bank."

"Oliver was bonded, so rest easy on that account. We have a chance to pull ourselves out of this."

"After Christmas you'll find a well-paying position," Claire assured me.

"I hope so. Kitty Wenzel threatened to thwart my efforts in that area."

Then I explained the conversation Kitty Wenzel and I had had the night before, omitting the portion about my homosexuality. Claire was tickled at the thought of our buying Oliver's mistress a house.

"Perhaps a tent, Strut. We could afford a small tent, couldn't we?"

"A very small tent," I smiled. "The dilemma is, presuming she was telling the truth, and I believe she was, what has happened to more than two hundred thousand dollars."

"Who knows, darling?" Claire said, her eyes twinkling. "Maybe Oliver put it in a Swiss bank!"

"Then I'll dispatch you tomorrow for Switzerland to retrieve it!" I teased.

Claire left me in order to continue cleaning. After writing a check for the heating bill, I glanced at the mantle clock and wondered if Vic had arrived in Norfolk yet. It was possible, but he did, after all, need some time with his family.

An hour later Kei wanted me to go to "our" room with him. His suitcases were open on the floor, his clothes spilling out into the room. He understandably wanted to put them away in drawers and closets, but my apparel was still there. He was impatient, pleading with me to move the furniture right after the funeral tomorrow. I agreed.

Sitting on the edge of the bed, I patted the space beside me, and Kei sat there. I had to discuss a situation that would be disheartening for him.

He was a student at Cornelius Calvert School For Boys, as I had been some years ago. It was the local day school for the rich and the privileged, and it enjoyed an excellent academic reputation.

"This is an unpleasant thing to have to tell you," I said, "but you will have to go to public school after Christmas."

"Leave Calvert?" He was surprised.

"Yes, I'm sorry, Kei." The disappointment on his face stung me. "It isn't something I want you to do. We cannot afford Calvert."

"It's okay," he said, swallowing hard. "I can handle it if I have to, Strut. Claire said that you're quitting school...leaving Washington and Lee, I mean...because you have to stay here to take care of us."

"For the same reason. To be blunt, there just isn't any money."

"When you get a good job, I can go back to Calvert, can't I?"

"When I can afford Calvert, I promise to re-enroll you, but the truth is, I do not know when that will be."

Kei nodded his head slowly. Then he gave me a hug and hurried off. I'm sure some tears were shed in private.

I thought again of Vic, yearned to see him, and my anticipation increased so that, by five o'clock, all of my reserve melted and I dialed his home. A maid answered and said that Vic was out. She was vague, as servants often are, but I gathered he had returned from Lexington and then gone out again. All I could do was to leave word for him to call me. Perhaps he was on his way over now.

By seven, having shaved, bathed, and dressed, I walked into the drawing room, which was large and furnished with French pieces that my grandmother had purchased during her visit in Paris. The furniture was arranged in small groupings, so that private conversations were discreetly possible.

There would be no need for such tonight.

Claire and Kei were already there. She wore a beige dress with a single strand of pearls, and Kei resembled a miniature man in his navy blue suit and tie. Claire asked if Vic had called, and I shook my head.

At seven fifteen Mrs. O'Brian showed in Jessica Cobb, and we stood to receive her. She gave all three of us little hugs before seating herself in an Empire chair.

"Strutwick, you are a tower of strength. Claire tells me that you stepped into Oliver's shoes without hesitation."

Miss Jessica Cobb, at seventy-three, was a gray-haired, tall and sturdy woman who exemplified old South charm. She was the principal survivor of an illustrious family almost as old as ours.

Unlike the Widdicombes, however, the Cobbs had ceased long ago to be identified with one particular residence. She lived alone in the Selden Apartments with a full-time domestic servant and a part-time chauffeur.

"You are kind." I smiled at the spinster. "How well I can manage remains to be seen."

"Coffee or tea, Jessie?" Claire asked, going to the silver service that Mrs. O'Brian had placed on a Louis XVI console earlier.

The two women chatted, Claire explaining to her older friend that she intended to convert Oliver's bedroom into a second floor parlor for herself.

"There are rooms on the third floor stuffed with family furniture, Jessie. On no account will I purchase new pieces."

"Good gracious, no, Claire. You have family heirlooms upstairs, superior to anything in the shops today. Just pick and choose carefully, and your lady's parlor will be lovely. Why, Carolyn can help you. She has good taste. It would help to take her mind off her daddy."

Claire explained to Jessie about Owen's withdrawal from the family, the impending divorce, and Carolyn's refusal to leave her room. Jessie straightened her back and acquired a serious expression.

"Carolyn can't mend things by thinking. It takes doing. Why, Carolyn's just dwelling on spent illusions. She needs to get out of that room."

"And she looks mighty peaked," Claire added. "Once the funeral is behind us, Strut and I will devote our energies to helping her."

"Why, my Aunt Pauline did the same thing. Her suitor died of influenza when Aunt Pauline was only twenty."

Jessie interrupted her tale to refill her coffee cup. She was a born storyteller, and we waited for her to resume the story. Even Kei was attentive.

"Well, poor Aunt Pauline was grief-stricken and would not leave her room." Jessie rolled her eyes heavenward. "Nobody in the family knew how she first got it, but the sorrowing woman started taking morphine. I remember one particular servant was suspected of bringing her the devil's sedative."

"What's morphine?" Kei asked.

"It is a drug used for people in great pain," I said. "It's usually administered only to those who are terminally ill because it is very addictive and dangerous."

"Wow! Did your Aunt Pauline get hooked, Miss Cobb?" Kei asked.

"Hooked? Well, we might say that about poor Pauline. By the time the family discovered she was using morphine, she certainly was, ah, hooked." Jessie made a gesture of despair with her free hand and shrugged her shoulders.

"How did she act, crazy-like?" Kei was interested. "Did she do all sorts of wild stuff?"

"Oh, mercy, no, my dear. She was as serene and sweet as she could be. And granddaddy just had to keep buying morphine for her. One thing didn't change, though...she continued to seclude herself in her room most of the time. I was the only person in the family who visited her there on a regular basis. She took pleasure in my company."

"What did she talk about?" Kei asked.

"My, did she ever have some queer notions! But, remember, I was a very young girl at the time. Oh, Aunt Pauline planned trips for the two of us, trips to India to see the Taj Mahal, to England to dine with the royal family." There was a musical lilt in Jessie's voice as she reminisced. "Toward the end she didn't leave her bed, but I still went to her, sat by her sickbed. Why, she gave me all her parasols, and some were lace! Aunt Pauline always had a generous heart. I'll remember her fondly to my dying day."

"Oh. Jessie, do you think Carolyn will end up like that?" Claire was uncomfortable with the prospect.

"No, dear, I don't think she could get the morphine if she wanted it. More likely Carolyn would flee from the house...to rejoin her true love."

"Go to Owen?" I was surprised. "We would not allow it. Furthermore, Owen wants the divorce."

"Not allow it? Strutwick, there is no such thing! I recollect my Papa saying those very words when he forbade my sister, Lillian, to see Gerald Peyton. Oh, didn't we have a time at our house over that man!"

"I think life was exciting back in those days," Kei exclaimed.

"You may be correct, Keith. In any case, Lillian—the family called her Lily—fell head over heels in love with this no-account Mr. Peyton."

"No-account?" I repeated. "Why then did Miss Cobb show him any attention if he were no-account?"

"He wasn't white trash at all, came from old Tidewater aristocracy, you might say. Gerald Peyton's great grandfather had made a fortune in merchant shipping, and his grandchildren were spoiled rotten. Gerald Peyton's father made a religion of serious drinking, ended up dying of cirrhosis of the liver."

Claire got up and refilled our cups. Hearing Jessica Cobb talk about years long-since gone sent my mind back through time to glimpses into a world that was no more. Even Kei, at eleven, had some awareness of this.

"My dear sister Lily had so many beaux, but she took just one seriously...Gerald Peyton, who was mighty handsome with his curly blond hair and that great big ingratiating grin. Lily adored him, but he was a compulsive gambler and owed money to half the men in Norfolk."

"Rags to rags in four generations," Claire interjected.

"Yes, that was true of the Peyton family. Well, mercy me, Papa hit the ceiling when Mr. Peyton requested Lily's hand in marriage! Papa ordered him off the premises, told him to stay away from Lily. Then Papa forbade Lily to be in touch with Mr. Peyton, referred to him as that wastrel!"

"That's not a good ending, Miss Cobb," Kei said. Apparently he had hoped for a happy conclusion.

"Dear boy, that is not the end. I only had to catch my breath. Lily was just as sassy as you please! She defied Papa and exchanged love letters with Mr. Peyton. Servants carried them back and forth, behind Papa's back. Then one night Mr. Peyton slipped up the veranda stairs and into Lily's bedroom. Papa was deaf as a doornail, anyway. The lovers stole away and eloped that very night, moved to New York City."

"Neat!" Kei declared. "The story *does* have a happy ending!"

"No, not really, Keith. Papa disowned Lily, forbade her to return to Norfolk. He vowed he would tar and feather Mr. Peyton if he ever came near Tidewater, and he didn't. They stayed in New York."

Keith's face fell. It was his introduction to Norfolk lore where his family had played a major role in history.

"My girlhood friend, Ethel Lanier, received letters for me from Lily, and I used Ethel's address to write back. I never told Papa about that correspondence, and Ethel's father didn't like Papa, so I was safe there." She sighed but continued.

"Lily and Mr. Peyton were happy together at first, but he started drinking heavily whenever he suffered gambling losses. Sometimes the young couple was penniless, living in one room. I thought they would end up in the poor house! Lily wrote that, when he was drunk, Mr. Peyton was the meanest man that ever drew breath!

"She got mighty frail. I really think she didn't have enough to eat. Poor Lily finally died of tuberculosis."

"One should not have to suffer because of love." I felt angry.

"But sometimes there is no help for it," Jessie answered me.

Just then Mrs. O'Brian ushered in Neil and Claire went to him, kissing him on the cheek. He was introduced to Kei and Jessie Cobb who remembered having known his grandmother at Saint Paul's.

After we sat down, Neil started a conversation with Kei about basketball. The boy liked him immediately. I was pleased that they could enjoy each other's company.

Our little group talked amiably, and no one mentioned Oliver Hall's death. At eight forty-five both Jessie Cobb and Neil Rice bade us good night. I excused myself and left Claire and Kei.

Closing myself in the library, I sat down behind the desk. Worried, I ran my hands through my hair, rumpling it. The room was quiet except for the incessant ticking of the clock which became needles stabbing my brain, sharp painful thrusts that pierced my soul.

Vic Gilmore had had ample time to phone me. Furthermore, he should have visited us tonight. The visitation hours had appeared in Oliver's obituary. Something was very wrong. I dialed the Gilmore residence.

Again a maid answered, and, when I asked to speak to Vic, she said to hold. In moments Mrs. Gilmore came on the line.

"Strutwick, dear, I was so distressed to hear of your father's death. I'm thinking about you all. Tell Claire that my prayers are for her, for all of you."

"Thank you, Mrs. Gilmore. We both appreciate your concern. We are coping with Oliver's unfortunate suicide and also with his foolish misdeed."

I could hear her gasp. The embezzlement was definitely a subject she wished to avoid.

"I would like very much to speak to Vic," I continued. "I have been eager to talk to him during this ordeal."

"I'd like to put him on the phone, Strutwick, but he has already gone to bed," she spoke too sweetly. "I know you understand. The boy's exhausted from his exams and the trip home."

"Then I'd like to catch him tomorrow morning. How early can I call?"

"Tomorrow's not good, I'm afraid. He'll be busy tomorrow, helping me with last minute Christmas shopping. I'm so behind this year. We'll be out most of the day. But we are concerned about you and Claire. If there is anything I can do...."

"No, thank you, Mrs, Gilmore. If you cannot put Vic on the phone, then there's nothing else you can do. Goodnight."

My hand was shaking as I hung up. Vic and his family were embarrassed about their association with Oliver Hall's family. To be more accurate, Vic was ashamed of me. He was breaking the bond between us. I sat there for fifteen minutes, hoping Vic would phone me. He had to know about my calls; I knew he was not asleep.

Anguish began to swell inside of me. Then I started shaking violently. My throat constricted, and I felt hot. Jumping up, I dashed from the library and up the staircase. I almost went into my bedroom, but I stopped. I had to be alone, and Kei would be coming up to bed. I fled down the hall and into a guest bedroom. Latching the door from the inside, I collapsed onto the bed. I wept out of control, hard sobs racking my body.

Vic Gilmore had been the nucleus of my world, the man I worshiped and cherished. We had become lovers in our Calvert School days, and I had never been unfaithful to him. I knew he would never again enfold me in his wonderful embrace. Vic, so gentle yet so strong, had broken away, did not want me any longer. Damn Oliver!

There in the darkness of the unused room I emptied myself of tears. When there were no more, a dry heaving punished me further. Then I grew calm but my head was splitting. I did not know how long I had been closed up there.

I stood and walked to the window. Needing fresh air, I opened it a little and then dropped into an armchair. The chilly air felt good, helped my throbbing head.

I heard footsteps in the hall. They stopped outside the room. Someone was listening. Presently the person moved away.

Taking stock of myself, I was incredulous as to my behavior. Never in my life had I cried with such abandonment. I was known as that Widdicombe boy who was so full of pride and sparkle.

It had been weak of me to love Victor Gilmore so intensely, foolish for me to invest my emotional strength in him. Henceforth, I would rely on only myself; others could desert me, and it would not matter. In that moment I swore that I would never cry again, almost spitting the words through clenched teeth. Any remaining vestige of boyhood left me forever.

I turned on the lamp beside my chair. The Tiffany was bronze and of a nautilus shell motif. Museum quality, Claire had once said. The house was packed with such treasures. These are the things that endure, and it was such tangible possessions as these that I would do anything to retain.

Needing aspirin, I went quietly to the hall bathroom and found them. The house was still...my house, with its beautiful old china and silver, graceful antique furniture, and carpets and oriental rugs without equal.

Going down the servants stairs, I went outside through the French doors in the family dining room. It was cold, and I could see my breath when I exhaled. Moonlight cast an enchanted aura over the courtyard.

Looking up at the house, I knew instinctively it was my legacy. Ownership of Widdicombe House might not be of great importance to some people, but there was more than one millionaire in Tidewater that could not gain admittance through even its rear entrance.

My teeth began to chatter, but my brain was totally clear now. Holding my head up proudly, I entered the house and climbed the stairs. From an inner conviction I knew that I would keep the

Widdicombe family in this grand old house. The family and the house...were inseparable. If separated, neither would be of great consequence.

When I crept into Kei's room, he was sleeping soundly. I stripped to undershorts and managed to get under the covers of the massive bed without waking him.

Claire, who could not even balance a bank statement, and Kei, who was cooperative about leaving the school lie loved...both of them had placed their faith in me to take care of them. I intended to make one hell of an attempt.

CHAPTER FOUR

"'I am the resurrection and the life, saith the Lord; he that believeth in me, though he were dead, yet shall he live: and whosoever liveth and believeth in me, shall never die.'"

Sitting between Kei and Claire in the front pew, I tried to concentrate on the service. Dry-eyed Claire looked very regal in her sable coat. My nephew concentrated on every word of the service. Jessica Cobb and Neil Rice sat directly behind us in the second row. Behind them were Judith Trilling, my age, and her mother. They were also members of Saint Paul's. The seven of us must have appeared infinitesimal in the immense nave.

"'We brought nothing into this world, and it is certain we can carry nothing out. The Lord gave, and the Lord hath taken away; blessed be the name of the Lord.'"

Oliver must have broken a rule, I mused to myself. It seemed that he had carried a large sum of money out of this world with him. When the service concluded, the hearse motored slowly to the cemetery. Directly behind Claire, Kei and I were chauffeured in the funeral home's black limousine. We were followed by Jessica Cobb in her chauffeured car, then there was Neil, and finally the Trillings.

"'Unto Almighty God we commend the soul of our brother departed, and we commit his body to the ground; earth to earth, ashes to ashes, dust to dust...'"

It was a bleak day, and only when the casket was lowered into the ground and the service was finished did I become interested in the people around me. I had experienced a degree of sadness during the graveyard rites. In spite of the problems Oliver had created, he had been a generous provider for many years. I was learning to respect that.

Jessie and Neil approached us, as did the Trillings, all offering comforting words. Claire thanked Judith and her mother for the food they had sent us that morning.

"Oh, so much fried chicken, really!" Claire spoke vivaciously.

"And mounds of potato salad, and Parker House rolls! Why, it's a feast!"

"We wanted to do more," Mrs. Trilling responded. "One does not always know just what's best to do at times like this."

"Old loyalties are important to us," Judith Trilling smiled at me. "There have been Widdicombes at Saint Paul's since Norfolk came into being. We revere your family."

I liked this striking young woman. She combined beauty, intelligence, and keenness. If she hadn't been Episcopalian, I might not have known her, but her name had been continually brought up by Claire and Jessie Cobb. Oliver had spoken glowingly of her, too.

Finishing high school the same year I graduated from Calvert, Judith Trilling had gone into real estate and was highly successful. She had taken other courses, obtaining her broker's license. In the past several months she had moved into commercial properties and was now making her mark in that field. Oliver had once said that she was the brightest person in Tidewater in real estate.

"But achievers like you are more important than family relics, Judith," I answered. "If I had your business acumen, my major problems would be over."

"Thank you, Strutwick. I'd say both achievement and ancestry are valuable." After a pause she added with a twinkle in her eyes, "And paired together they form a very superior combination."

I laughed and for some reason did not sense any heterosexual aggressiveness in her words. Instead, I felt a kinship with her, a feeling of support, and I did not understand why. It was as though we shared some secret.

"Carolyn isn't here," Mrs. Trilling declared, suddenly realizing my sister's absence. "Is she all right?"

"The poor girl has taken to her bed," Jessie answered for us.

"Owen has left." Claire was blasé. "The rooster has flown the coop."

"My object of curiosity is Mrs. Kitty 'Wenzel." I said, following Claire's lead. "She, too, is conspicuous by her absence."

"Perhaps she's out house-hunting today." Claire offered.

Mrs. Trilling's face registered polite shock, and she put one gloved hand to her mouth. Judith, after a quick glance at Claire and me, smiled knowingly.

Once home I checked with Mrs. O'Brian who reported that Carolyn had slept most of the afternoon. Then Kei and I changed to casual clothes. That morning I had asked Neil to help in moving the furniture, and he arrived, bringing two day laborers with him.

Neil looked more appealing to me than he had before. Once he removed his jacket, it was obvious that he was dressed for work in tee shirt and jeans. His chest was more developed than I would have guessed, and his arms looked strong in a sinewy way. The pants were tight, outlining muscular legs. They were cuffed up to reveal white socks and the tops of his laced-up work-boots. Without his usual buttoned-down look, I felt attracted to him.

From the third floor storage rooms we brought down a large Victorian armoire, putting it in the family living room. Then we carried my bedroom furniture down to the room. All the living room furniture went into storage on the third floor. Among the stored pieces there I discovered a dark sofa of top-grain leather with brass nailhead trim that I liked very much. We made space for it in my "new" first-floor bedroom.

Next we moved Oliver's bedroom furniture into my old room which was now Kei's. When I saw him carrying a china clock from Oliver's room, I stopped him.

"That clock was in my bedroom when I was a boy. I always loved it."

The clock was French with graceful curves. Hand-painted on it's fine white china were a rural French scene and many small flowers.

"Oliver liked it, too." Claire, on hearing us, came into the room. "He took it out of your room for himself...years ago. But it doesn't keep time anymore."

"I'll take it down to your room, Strut," Kei offered. "You can get it fixed."

"Someday." I thanked Kei, and he carried it downstairs.

In the third-floor storage rooms, Claire directed the four of us as to which pieces to carry down to her second-floor lady's parlor. Kei was in his bedroom, putting away his things, apparently having forgotten that he had intended to search the house from top to bottom. He missed his chance.

"Have you seen these, Strut?" Claire called out, going to large cloth-covered frames propped against one side of the room. "The family portraits."

Neil and I joined her. I was intrigued, not even remembering we had family portraits.

"This is my father, Cedric Widdicombe," she said, lifting the protective cloth from a picture of a gray-haired gentleman.

"You favor him slightly, Claire," I smiled. "Around the eyes."

"And this is Gerald, grandson of John Widdicombe, who started the American branch," Claire continued.

"The American *dynasty* of Widdicombes," Neil corrected her gently.

"Note that red hair," I added, "The primary Widdicombe characteristic!"

"There are more portraits," Claire said. "Should we hang them again?"

"Again?" I was puzzled.

"They once hung along the front staircase. Oliver had them brought up here."

We took the portraits downstairs and, while we still had Neil and the laborers, hung them on the wall along the curved staircase between the first and second floors. We began at the bottom and worked up. When we were through, there was still room for two more. My private hope was that someday Kei and I would have our portraits hanging in these spaces. Finally the work was over, and Neil fetched his jacket.

"We will eat after you take the men back." Claire touched him on the arm.

"But I'm not fit company, ma'am," Neil protested. "I'm sweaty and sticky."

"A touch of masculine body aroma is...ah, interesting," I smiled, winking at him. "Please return and enjoy the Trilling's fried chicken with us. Afterwards we can talk, just the two of us."

"Yes, do, Neil," Claire insisted, "and I'll try to get Carolyn to join us. Now that the funeral is behind us, I shall devote myself to helping my daughter. Any help from friends is welcomed."

Mrs. O'Brian heated the chicken and rolls, and, when Neil returned, I sat down at the head of the table. Neil was next to me, and Claire seated herself at the other end, Kei beside her.

"Carolyn *is* coming down," Claire almost whispered. "Now no one is to mention Owen or Oliver."

Fifteen minutes after Mrs. O'Brian had served us, Carolyn burst into the family dining room, her red hair askew and her green negligee disheveled. She stared at us strangely.

"Mother!" Kei exclaimed.

"There you sit, Keith Fleming, not ready to leave, and you know your father is on his way over to pick us up! People will think I haven't taught you any manners! There's so much to do at home, Claire, with my bridge club coming tomorrow afternoon and the house a sight! Owen is immaculate and expects the same high standards of me! Why, the boys are so messy and unruly that I practically have to force them to pick up after themselves! Three rowdy boys on my hands, and good help is impossible to find! Where is Father? Working to all hours again, I suppose!"

Carolyn flitted about the room nervously, talking nonstop.

"Indeed, he puts us all to shame, the long hours he works! Keith! What is the matter with you? I told you to get your coat! Your father will be here any minute! I don't know why the Lord couldn't have given me three sweet obedient daughters!"

Kei started to cry. I had to remind myself that he was still a child. Claire, looking frightened, reached out and put her arm around him comfortingly. Carolyn continued to babble, storming around the room. Then her eyes fixed on Neil.

"And who are you? You're not Owen! I suppose you are that Victor Gilmore that Strutwick is always talking about. Well, you look grimy, and your clothes are dirty! A fine example to set for my little Keith, coming to the table like that! Strutwick, I must say, you do not look any cleaner! I don't know what this family is coming to! I'd not seat either of you at my table, looking the way you do! Where *is* Owen? He always keeps me waiting! If he doesn't come in the next few minutes, I'll call a taxi! I don't want to stay in this old house any longer! Owen said he—"

"Come, Carolyn, let me help you," I said, going to her. "I'll help you get ready."

Mrs. O'Brian had heard Carolyn from the kitchen, and she came to help. With one of us on each side of her, we guided Carolyn out of the family dining room, through the hall, and toward the stairs.

"Why, thank you, Strutwick, your concern is appreciated, I must say! And Mrs. O'Brian, dear Mrs. O'Brian! Always like a mother to me! Sometimes I think you are the only one who gives a damn about me around this old house! The *only* one! And, Strutwick, I don't mean to say you're not nice, but I see so little of you. Why, it's as if you reside on another planet!"

Carolyn continued talking incessantly, but she was exhausting herself. She leaned heavily on me as we climbed the stairs.

"There, there, Miss Carolyn, you are gonna wear yourself out before Mister Owen gets here to pick you up." Mrs. O'Brian soothed. "He's expecting you to be ready for dinner and dancing at the club tonight. No sense in tiring yourself like this."

"Yes, I *am* tiring, and I should be fresh for Owen. I should nap, I suppose. What time will he pick me up?"

We managed to get her to her room and onto her bed. As soon as her head touched the pillows, she ceased talking. Stretching, she looked at us suspiciously and then fell asleep.

"You go downstairs and call a doctor, Mister Strutwick. Miss Carolyn needs help fast! I'll stay with her."

In the family dining room I found Claire crying as she searched a booklet for the doctor's home phone number. Kei was weeping on Neil's shoulder.

"I'm looking for old Dr. Ewell's number," Claire sobbed. "Carolyn has to have professional attention tonight!"

"She's lost touch with reality, Claire," I said.

"Shh...the boy!" Claire inclined her head toward Kei.

"He knows. He heard her."

I went over to Kei and Neil, and Claire got up and went to the kitchen phone. Running my fingers through the boy's hair, I thought to myself that our difficulties were multiplying. Even though I had never been close to Carolyn, this scene of hers wrenched my heart. Her lifestyle had been destroyed by Owen's abandonment of her, and she could not cope.

Kei let go of Neil and threw his arms around me. I hugged him tightly, searching for the right words to comfort him.

"Kei, I can't tell you that your mother is going to be all right because I don't know. After the doctor sees her, we will understand better." He looked up at me with his red and swollen eyes. "I can tell you that I will take care of you. I promise you that."

He calmed down as I patted his shoulders. Neil and I looked at each other. This man was a gem, I knew, and he was also drawn to me. Furthermore, he was masculine and somewhat appealing. I resolved to make him my lover. I needed his emotional support, and, being honest with myself, I knew I needed a bed partner, a man to give me sexual fulfillment. I did not intend to do without that.

"Dr. Ewell is on his way over, Strut."

Claire, Kei, Neil, and I waited in her "new" lady's parlor while Dr. Ewell was with Carolyn, Mrs. O'Brian in attendance. We had explained Carolyn's verbal outburst and irrational thinking to the doctor.

"I think I am in the way here, Strut. I'll go home. You can call me if you need me."

"No, Neil, stay!" I stood up. "1 want you here. We need to talk."

When Dr. Ewell joined us, he assured us that Carolyn should rest now, that he had given her a sedative. He instructed us, however, to have someone with her at all times, to be on the safe side. We were to have her in his office at eight o'clock Monday morning. lie would have another doctor and two psychiatrists there for a thorough evaluation.

A subdued Kei walked Dr. Ewell to the front door, while we worked out our shifts. Mrs. O'Brian, still in Carolyn's room, would be first, with Claire relieving her at midnight. I would step in about four a.m. Each of us could nap in the wing chair beside Carolyn's bed. Neil offered to take a turn in the late morning; his offer was accepted.

"I should not have made light of Owen's leaving, Strut." Claire was contrite, as she brought Neil and me glasses of her port. "I feel so ashamed. He means the world to Carolyn."

"No self-recriminations, Claire," I soothed her. "You did not say anything in front of Carolyn."

"No, I don't think I did. But I am very worried. There is a strain of madness in the family."

Neil and I were both shocked.

"Oh, all the older citizens of Norfolk know that. My great uncle,

Dalton Widdicombe, went mad, mad as a hatter! Spent his last years up on the third floor. A manservant was always with him."

"If what you are saying is true, and I certainly don't doubt you, dear Claire, then any traumatic event could have done this to Carolyn?" I asked, regaining my composure.

"Oh, yes, I believe you are right. "Every now and then a Widdicombe just plunges into insanity. It's an inherited trait, or something like that."

Claire had spoken so innocently and so sincerely that both Neil and I grinned.

"We Widdicombes are a curious breed," I remembered aloud.

At that moment Kei came in. He was drinking a Coke.

"Come sit by me, precious," Claire said, patting the place next to her on the loveseat. "Where have you been?"

"In the kitchen. I put the food away and washed the dishes."

"Thank you, Kei," I smiled at the boy. "We are a truly united family. We'll do just fine."

"I needed something to do."

"Are you all right?" I asked him.

"Sure, I guess so. Mother's in a bad way, but I'll always love her, even if she does think I'm a lot of trouble."

"She doesn't think that at all, Kei," Claire said, putting her arm around him. "She is ill. When she's better..."

"Maybe she won't get better. She's gone crazy—I know that."

"We'll see, Kei, we'll see," Claire said softly.

"But I love you and Strut. I know you'll take care of me," he said.

"I will always be there for you," I told him. "You are not only my flesh and blood, you are our family's future." He looked at me seriously for a moment.

"I think I'll turn in now." Kei changed the subject. "I'm tired. You know, this is my first night alone in my own room."

As he left, he kissed Claire and me goodnight and shook hands with Neil. I watched him square his little shoulders and disappear through the door.

"Inner strength there," I told Claire and Neil.

After finishing our wine, Neil and I went to my downstairs bedroom. Claire needed to rest before her shift with Carolyn. I thanked Neil for his help and support and told him that I needed him. I had decided to seduce the man tonight,

"I am going to go upstairs and shower," I said. "Will you wait here for me? We haven't had any time alone. Something good has to come out or this wretched day."

Neil assured me that he would wait, and, grabbing up my bathrobe, I left him sitting on the leather sofa. When 1 returned, 1 tossed my dirty clothes into a hamper and went to him.

"Neil, do you remember what I said in your office yesterday? About never hiding the fact that I am a homosexual?"

"Why, uh, yes," he hesitated and blushed. "I remember, Strut."

"Claire realizes it, although we don't discuss it. She simply accepts."

"I accept you, too, Strut," he responded, looking into my eyes.

"Unless I am losing *my* mind, I believe you are gay, too." I put my hand on his face, stroking his cheek, cupping his chin. "Am I correct?"

We were silent, with only the sound of his heavy breathing between us. I bent my head and kissed his forehead. As I did, my robe fell open, and I knew he was staring at my hardening manhood.

"I want you, Neil," I whispered and kissed him on the lips, softly, slowly.

"Yes, Strut, I am, of course I am," he exclaimed, standing up and taking me in his arms. "I'm just like you, only not as brave about it!"

"Let me teach you not to be shy!"

I put my arms around his neck and captured his mouth with mine. Kissing him hard, my tongue probed, working its way inside his mouth. His embrace was strong, and I reveled in his strength, feeling his excitement pressing through his trousers and against me. Then I broke from the kiss and my mouth found his ear. My tongue entered it. Warm bursts of pleasure shot through the man, and his breathing became rough.

Having aroused his passion, I broke from his embrace and guided him to my bed, pushing him onto it. As he lay there, I could see his rigidity straining against the fabric of his trousers.

"The door!" he cried out. "Lock the door!"

I leaned over and ran my hand inside his shirt. His chest was hairy, his nipples hard. Then I stopped and locked both doors to the room. Returning to the bedside, I let my robe slip off my shoulders and fall to the floor. Neil spread his arms, wanting to pull me onto the bed with him.

"Easy, easy," I admonished gently. "We will go slowly. This is our first time. I want to cherish every moment."

I sat on the foot of the bed and rested one hand on his thigh. The cuffs of his trouser legs had worked up, exposing flesh above his white socks. With my other hand I ran my fingers gently over the hairs there. They curled under my touch.

"My god, I love you!" Neil uttered hoarsely. "I've loved you for years!"

Moving my hand from his thigh, I unfastened his belt buckle. I worked his zipper down. Slowly I probed with my fingers inside. He trembled.

I was going to enjoy this. Neil wasn't exactly a virgin, but he was inexperienced in true lovemaking. I knew I would be an excellent teacher.

In the morning I woke up feeling good. It was late, but I had spent hours in Carolyn's room before retiring and had found it impossible to relax there. Poor lost Carolyn. The entire structure upon which she had built her life was gone, and it had been too much for her to accept.

Neil had floated out of my bedroom on clouds of rapture. Prior to our making love, he had experienced only anonymous sex. He had met strangers for lonely one-night stands. It was rough sexual gratification only. He did not dare so much as to give them his real name. He feared associating his homosexuality with his work and his home. That kind of sex never fulfilled, never satisfied. But Neil's life had changed last night in my bed. He had fallen in love with me. Neil was mine now; he adored me.

I smiled drowsily, getting out of bed and going to my door that led into the walled garden. I opened it, and the frigid air immediately chilled my naked body. Snowflakes were falling in the garden, the kind that melt as they touch the ground. The invigorating air rendered me totally awake and I quickly closed the door. Slipping into clothes and socks, I stepped into the hall, black coffee on my mind. I heard voices, excited and loud. They were arguing.

"Let go of my arm! You are not my keeper! I'm going to Owen!"

"Come back to your room, Carolyn! Owen isn't down there! You are over-wrought!"

"I tell you I hear Owen blowing the horn in his car, you idiot! Release me! I'm going to Owen!"

It was Carolyn and Claire, and I followed the sounds to the front staircase. Standing at the foot of the stairs, I looked up and to see them struggling at the top. Claire was trying to pull Carolyn back toward her bedroom.

"Carolyn! Stop it!" I shouted.

"Strutwick! Call Owen in here!" Carolyn screamed.

She lurched, shoving Claire down behind her. Then Carolyn pitched forward, hurling head-first down the stairs. There was a sickening snap as she tumbled, almost in a ball, down the entire circular staircase, landing in a heap at my feet.

As I bent over her, Claire rushed down the stairs, and Kei and Mrs. O'Brian came running from the kitchen.

"Someone call an ambulance!" Claire screamed.

Kei threw his arms around Carolyn, crying wildly. As I bent over her still body, I sensed from the impossible position of her head that her neck was broken. I got to my feet and pulled Kei away from her, cradling him in my arms. I could hear Mrs. O'Brian shouting into the telephone, but I knew that Carolyn had found release from her agony.

CHAPTER FIVE

"Strut, dear, I don't want you to be discouraged." Claire soothed. "There has to be a position for you."

It was three in the afternoon, and we were having coffee in Claire's lady's parlor on the second floor. A cold March wind was blowing. Even through the closed windows we could hear it rustling in the trees.

"Discouraged? To seek employment for two and a half months without success *is* discouraging, but I'm no quitter." I emptied my Haviland cup and stood up. Walking to a window, I pulled back the lace curtain. Tree branches were whipping angrily. "Do you think Kitty Wenzel followed through on her threat to blackball me in the business community?"

"I have no doubt at all," Claire answered. "According to Jessie, Kitty and Oliver entertained business friends of his in her apartment."

"And she was semi-accepted by them." I left the window and sat down beside Claire. She poured more coffee in my cup and I sipped it as I talked. "She did her dirty work and then left town."

"We know she moved her furnishings from the Selden Apartments on the very day of Oliver's funeral," Claire said. "Wouldn't tell the doorman her destination, either. That isn't exactly the way an honest woman conducts herself."

"Well, that's in the past." I finished my coffee and stood up to go. "We have had our good fortune, too. Neil moved in, and his financial aid toward household expenses has been a blessing. Furthermore, all the legal papers on Kei are finalized. The court declared he is fully in your custody."

"And after all he endured, he has made an excellent adjustment." Claire smiled.

"A resilient young man." I stopped in the doorway. "lie even *likes* public school."

I left, going to my room on the first floor to lie down before Neil came home. I wanted to look fresh for him.

Carolyn's death had incapacitated all four of us. Kei and Mrs. O'Brian had wept and tried to comfort each other. For the first time I saw that capable woman lose her grip. Claire took to her bed. As for myself, I fought back tears, determined not to shed then. I felt numb and was unable to make decisions right then.

I discovered that, although I did not like Carolyn very much, I had loved her. She was my sister and of my blood. Her death occurring so quickly after Oliver's deepened the sorrow.

Neil and Jessie Cobb stayed with us around the clock for almost a week. Jessie had canceled a Christmas visit with cousins in Alexandria to be with Claire. Neil supported me both emotionally and physically.

In the end Claire, Kei, Mrs. O'Brian, and I coped by not mentioning Carolyn's name. After the funeral this was usually possible.

Convincing Neil to move into Widdicombe house was not difficult. He was in love with me. He chose Carolyn's bedroom for himself, attempting to erase for us the ache of her last few days in there. To some extent it worked. Had he selected one of the other bedrooms, we might have closed Carolyn's room off indefinitely.

After Carolyn's funeral, Neil and I made love most nights. He came downstairs to my room after the others were in bed. Although I enjoyed the sex, he was unimaginative in bed. The security of resting safely in his embrace afterwards was more precious. I needed the comfort and protective feeling he communicated to me.

Neil's income was modest. After taking his degree in accounting, he had worked for a large firm in Newport News. Once he had saved enough money to start his own business, he returned to Norfolk and opened the small one-man office a year and a half ago. Because he seldom missed a Sunday at Saint Paul's, I did not know he had lived out of town.

He contributed what he could to the household expenses, but it was not enough. My money was running out. Once I paid the real estate taxes, I would be stone-broke. I had to go to work in a matter of days. The family was economizing in every way it could.

Christmas had not been a festive occasion. Claire forsook her usual little Yuletide treats of fruitcake, marzipan, rum balls, and egg nog. We did have a turkey because poultry was inexpensive.

Don't count on anyone but yourself, I repeatedly vowed. Take any job available, any at all.

Neil was at his office the day my trunk arrived from college. My happiness at receiving the rest of my wardrobe turned to despair when I discovered Vic's worn bathrobe among my clothes. It had been packed in error. My heart ached as I held it up. Vic had loved it and had refused to throw it out. Slowly I slipped into it and was almost swallowed up, The ratty old terrycloth robe still retained Vic's body scent.

For a few moments my thoughts receded to the happy days when Vic and I had loved and cherished each other. I yearned for those days but fought for my grip on reality. My life was different now; I could not dwell on Vic. Removing the robe, I hung it on a hook at the back of my armoire. I have not touched it since.

Just a catnap before Neil arrived, I promised myself, and closed my bedroom door. Sitting down to take off my shoes, I was surprised by a knock on the door.

"Mister Strutwick, can I speak to you for a minute?" Mrs. O'Brian called. She came in and closed the door.

"Miss Charlotte sent me. She wants to speak to you."

"Aunt Charlotte?" I hadn't even thought of Aunt Charlotte hidden away on the third floor for a long time. "Is she ill?"

"Same as ever." Mrs. O'Brian smiled in a secretive way. "Miss Charlotte don't change."

"I wonder what she wants with me. I've never seen her in my life."

"You're the head of the Widdicombe family, ain't you? You better go tend to your great-aunt. Only thing else she told me was for you to keep it confidential."

I went directly to the third floor and knocked on Aunt Charlotte's door. My curiosity about this eighty-seven year old mystery relative was about to be satisfied.

"The door is unlocked," a squeaky voice called. "Come in."

Once inside everything was indistinct. The room was smoky. A thick blue-grey cloud enveloped an armchair situated near a window, and the waning sunlight did not help. As my eyes adjusted, I discerned a small figure seated in the chair, puffing on a cigarette.

"Turn on the lamps, Strutwick," she directed.

The lights helped. I perceived a little wrinkled woman wrapped in smoke, a cigarette in one hand and what seemed to be a glass of sherry in the other. She was wearing a plain black dress with one strand of pearls around her tiny neck and a multi colored shawl over her thin shoulders. The cloud of smoke remained around her, a cloud which she perpetually refueled with her Chesterfield.

"I hope you didn't expect some dignified spinster, young man? Sit down where I can see you, so we can talk."

"I apologize, Aunt Charlotte. I didn't intend to stare," I said, sitting in a nearby chair. "I didn't know what to expect."

"Dispense with the 'aunt,' please," she chirped. "I'm Charlotte Widdicombe, no more, no less. And I have the advantage, Strutwick. I have observed *you* in the garden many times...from my window, you see." She waved a bony, heavily-veined hand in its direction.

"Just Charlotte is fine with me," I responded, beginning to relax. "I have wanted to meet you for years."

"There has been no need...until now. You are, as I understand it, the head of the family now, and you are short of money, in need of a job."

"That's my situation. Badly in need of a job."

"Mrs. O'Brian keeps me informed...on everything. She's a fine girl, loyal and true to the family." She pushed back a wisp of grey hair from her face and reached for her glass of sherry.

"I will take any kind of work I can get," I stated flatly. "I'm too desperate to be particular."

"You shall have a job, young man, and you see that you make good at it." Charlotte alternated between puffing on her cigarette and sipping her sherry.

"I've written a note for you to take to Mr. Jarman at The Greene Room."

"The Greene Room?" I was surprised. It was a gay bar and had been in business for years and years. "I have never been there!"

"You will...this evening. You *are* homosexual; I already know that."

She spoke through the blue-grey cloud of smoke.

"Did Mrs. O'Brian tell you that, too?" I felt betrayed.

"She did not! I watched you in the garden, as I said...and in the gazebo you once kissed a tall man with dark hair."

I got up and went to the window. From there, Charlotte had an excellent view into the gazebo. "Did it embarrass you?" I asked, returning to my chair.

"Evidently you have not been told why I lived on the third floor in seclusion all these years, Strutwick."

"I have no idea. No one talks about you in my presence, Charlotte."

"Then it is high time you learned about me. When I was a young woman, I loved and lived with a teacher, Lydia Hooker. The family was horrified. Lydia was dearer to me than life itself. Then, at only twenty-four years of age, she was in a boating accident...in the Chesapeake Bay." Charlotte's thin lips quivered, and she raised a finger to them. "Lydia was drowned. My father and brother came to our little house for me...they made me return to Widdicombe House...forced me to stay on the third floor until I promised to marry an eligible bachelor." She stopped speaking and shook herself, as if to discard the bad memories. "That was in 1907, and I am not wed yet!"

I was dumbfounded. "My god, I understand now! As a lesbian, you were an embarrassment to the family, so they forced you home when you were most vulnerable, when your lover died!"

She nodded briefly "She was all I cared about in the world, so I did not mind being shut away up here...in time I learned to prefer it." Charlotte's voice was only a murmur. I sensed she was tiring.

"Do you wish for me to leave? Come back later?"

"No, stay. Give me...a few moments," she answered.

She finished her glass of sherry and I refilled her glass from the decanter on the table. As she sipped, her energy seemed to be restored.

"My priorities are different now...the family comes first."

She began again. "The Widdicombes and Widdicombe House must endure. Mr. Jarman will remember me, and he will employ you...make the most of this."

"Working with the public, and the gay public at that, will be a new experience for me."

"Never be too proud to mingle with the common people, Strutwick. They can be your salvation."

"1 shall be at Mr. Jarman's Greene Room before six o'clock. And

I shall not disappoint you."

She squinted at me for a moment. "There are givers and there are takers in this world." She lit another Chesterfield, her eyes remaining on me. "Which will you be?"

"I will learn to be a taker, Charlotte."

She nodded in approval. "The power in the name Widdicombe still exists. Preserve that," she said. Her shoulders sagged. "Now you must go...I am very tired. But come back to me in a week."

She pointed to a table by the door. On it was an envelope, and when I picked it up I could see only two words, "Bingo Jarman," on the face of it. Putting it in my shirt pocket, I went to the aged lady. Gently I raised one of her hands to my lips and kissed it. Her expression did not change. Then I left.

Descending to the second floor, I saw Neil in his room. Shutting us in, I told him all that had happened. "We don't tell the others?" he asked.

"No one, Neil. This is our secret." I smiled. "Will you cover for me while I go to The Greene Room? Tell Claire I am checking a job possibility."

"A lot transpires in this house behind closed doors," Neil mused.

Twenty-five minutes later I was walking in the front door of The Greene Room.

A man who appeared to be in his early thirties stopped me in the foyer. "Whoa, buddy, we're not open yet. Won't be 'til seven."

"I am not here as a customer." I handed him the envelope. "From an old friend. I'm to wait for a reply."

"Old friend?" The man looked at the envelope and then at me suspiciously. "All of Mr. Jarman's 'old friends' died a long time ago...before you were born, kid."

"Perhaps not all," I responded. "I'll wait."

Mumbling, the man opened the door near the front entrance and went up narrow stairs. While he was gone I had an opportunity to observe the place. It was on the seamy side, in need of a decorator's attention.

I was standing by a nondescript counter, and behind it was a wooden stool. Beyond the foyer was a long bar, with glasses on shelves behind it and only a few stools in front of it. Then there were a dozen or so tables with chairs, and at the far end was a raised platform for dancing. At one end of the platform was a glass booth for the disc jockey and his turntables. There were no windows.

A young man was wet-mopping the dance area. He looked up, smiled at me, and then continued working.

Presently the letter bearer returned and held open for me the door to the stairs. He beckoned silently for me to go up. Once I reached the top, I realized that the second floor was one large pink room with little light. At first I did not see anyone.

"Over here," a raspy voice called, and I turned toward the voice. "On the bed. Come here."

As I approached the bed, I perceived a small figure propped up on pillows. A gnarled hand waved me closer.

"I'm not very well today," the wrinkled old man said. "Stand close to the bed so I can see you. My damn eyes are not much good any more."

Looking at him, I was reminded of a drawing of Rumpelstiltskin in one of my children's books. Bingo Jarman was skinny with blue veins all over his bald head, his arms, and his legs. As I looked, he pulled his purple robe tighter around himself.

"Mr. Jarman?' I said, putting out my hand in greeting. He pushed it away.

"Shaking hands is for straight fuckers, not me! Kiss me on the forehead, please!"

I did and managed a smile.

"So, you are Charlotte's great-nephew! Well, well! I knew her when she was a young woman...and she was a beauty! That was before Dalton and Cedric Widdicombe put her in solitary confinement!"

Bingo Jarman appeared even more aged than did Charlotte. This was my day for meeting human antiquities.

"I know what you're thinking!" Bingo lashed out. "You are wondering how the hell old I am. The answer to ninety-two, and I am proud of every damn year!"

I decided there was no really appropriate response to that.

"Sir, I came to ask for a job. I need one badly."

"Don't think I am senile, youngster. My mind is still keen. I know why you came. Tony had to read the letter to me out loud, but that's because of my failing eyesight, not brain erosion!"

"Yes, sir."

"I hear the glorious old Widdicombe family has fallen on hard times!"

"Yes, some may say that, sir!" I flared.

"Well...you are a pretty boy, I'll admit that." Bingo calmed down. "Here, plump my pillows for me."

"Thank you for the compliment," I said, leaning over to rearrange his pillows. When I finished, I helped to ease the chalky-white old man into a more comfortable position.

"You have that red Widdicombe hair. At least I can see that good!" He cackled at his own words. "Tell me, are you a tity-boo, flitting from one endeavor to the next, from one man to the next?"

"No, sir. I have one lover, and he is all I want. And I won't 'flit' away from this endeavor, this bar. I will stay and work and remain loyal to you."

"I think you have Charlotte's qualities...stubbornness, loyalty, and pride. I like that."

"Stubbornness, loyalty, and pride are necessary to keep me going."

"You have the job. See Tony Pogue downstairs and tell him I said to put you to work tonight. Rut I warn you, there is no trading on old glory here. It is work, hard work, day after day after day."

"Yes, sir."

CHAPTER SIX

I was at my desk in the library, catching up on entries in the Widdicombe journals. The bar had kept me so busy that I sometimes neglected my duties as family historian. I wrote today's date, May 28, 1973, and wondered where the past three years had gone. Last year's name changes were already entered. I smiled as I remembered Claire's saying, "Since Oliver died, I feel like a Widdicombe again. I do believe I'll change my name back." Kei and I decided to follow suit. All three of us legally became Widdicombes. Discarded were the surnames of Hall and Fleming. We felt right, if not orthodox, about it.

Kei, at fourteen, was growing out of his clothes as fast as I bought them. Intuitively I had realized he would be a "member of the club" one day. The boy had gay tendencies and proclivities. I saw my younger self in him.

When he was twelve, he had wanted a pair of green silk pajamas like mine. I had said I didn't think they were right for him.

"But I want to be just like you," Kei had said.

"Never say that; don't even think it. The one thing you can do better than anyone else in the world is to be yourself," I answered. "So work on it and perfect it."

Evidently he had pondered over my words. His personality began to develop in a unique, charming manner. Moreover, he was becoming more masculine. He was starting quarterback on his junior high football team last autumn. Determined to have strong muscular bodies, Kei and Neil worked out together at the "Y" two nights a week.

I wished I loved Neil. Everything he did was for my benefit. I had been faithful to him and tried to feign love. Neither of us liked my working late hours at The Greene Room. We both liked sex too much to forego it, so I went to his room many early mornings, after I returned from the bar.

We had rehired maids and a gardener, and we were paying Mrs. O'Brian again. Kei's personal needs called for money. He was forever needing clothes and shoes. I bought myself some jeans and tee shirts for work; nothing more was needed. Claire had closets full of clothes. She did spend some money on dinners at the Botetourt Yacht and Country Club with Jessie Cobb. This was the only Widdicombe visibility in Norfolk society, so it was worth the expense. It took all that Neil and I made to pay the bills; there was nothing left over.

As I finished entering Kei's athletic endeavors in the journal, there was a knock on the library door and Kei came in.

"Mind it I interrupt you for a moment, Strut?" he asked.

"You may always have your moment, Kei. Rely on that."

He smiled and came behind the desk to stand by me. When he put his large hands on my shoulders, I felt paternal pride.

"Paying bills?"

"No, writing in the Widdicombe Journals. Paying bills is next."

"I'll be glad when I'm old enough to take some of the responsibility. You're always working."

"Do not wish your life away." I looked up at him and smiled. "Try to enjoy the now."

"I do. In fact, that's what I came in to ask about...the now."

"And the question?"

"The question is, can Bradley spend the night with me tonight? No school tomorrow, Strut."

"Bradley Boddicker? He was your friend back in Calvert, wasn't he?"

"Yeah. We were baby-buddies way back in the first grade."

"Good family, there," I said. Bradley was almost pretty, I remembered, and more effeminate than I was at that age. "Yes, by all means, have him spend the night...any time at all."

"Thanks, Strut. It means a lot to me."

I caught myself hoping that Kei and Brad were enjoying sex together. Kei kissed me on the forehead and, grinning lopsidedly, was gone.

The youngsters were fourteen, and Vic and I had begun at thirteen.

Vic Gilmore was an old wound that refused to heal. I loved and hated him simultaneously. I should have put him behind me, out of my mind, but couldn't. Now his forthcoming marriage to Marjorie

Thayer had been announced. She was very plain, very shy, and very wealthy. Perhaps Vic thought marriage would banish his homosexual inclinations, but I know it wouldn't. Jessie Cobb had received a wedding invitation, but Claire and I had not.

It was five o'clock, and I decided to make myself a drink. I left the library and made my way to the kitchen. Swinging the door partially open, I realized Kei was on the phone. I stopped, not wanting to intrude. He did not know I was there.

"Bradley, Strut says you can spend the night here any time...no, not every night!" Kei's voice dropped to a whisper. "You'd drain me dry! Yes, I'll want you forever, but not sex every night. At least not until I'm older and bigger."

Quietly I let the door swing shut and returned to the library. Maybe Kei's first love affair will endure, not be extinguished the way mine was. Seating myself behind the desk again, I reached for two bills for The Greene Room and thought about Bingo Jarman.

I liked him very much. He was a spunky old man who had retained his pride. At ninety-five this was just short of a miracle.

Bingo and Charlotte had been friends when they were young, and now shared similarities other than being elderly gay people. Both were wise, spirited, and both read the obituaries every day. Actually Max read them to Bingo because his eyesight was so poor he could not read anymore.

I had continued to visit Charlotte weekly. She gave good advice which helped me to mature. The last time we talked she told me, "Do not say all that you think." I had a tendency to blurt out too much too inappropriately. I worked on this flaw.

One late afternoon Charlotte passed away peacefully. dozing in her chair, a glass of sherry and a pack of Chesterfields on the table beside her. I would miss that grand old aristocrat for the rest of my life. I reflected on the changes she had wrought.

Three years ago I had no idea I would be managing a bar now. I had been naive and apprehensive my first night there. Only the dire need for money had made me stay.

"Mr. Jarman said to put me to work," I had told Tony Pogue, the bar manager.

"Oh, shit, another new guy to train," he muttered. "Hey, Max, get over here!"

The young man I had seen mopping the floor earlier hurried over and smiled at me again. He was small and had a baby face. This fellow had to be older than he looked.

"Show this guy the ropes, and teach him how to draw a fucking draft without a lot of head!" Tony ordered and then left us alone.

"I'm Max. Come on with me, and we'll start with the drafts." Max spoke almost sweetly. "Don't pay no attention to Tony. He's just a moody guy."

After the lessons in drawing drafts, Max had me take off my shirt. "Better to work in just your tee shirt...and wear jeans tomorrow. Tight ones if you got 'em. Bartenders here dress to look sexy, not fancy, but, heck, you didn't know."

Max did turn out to be a sweet guy. I learned he was twenty-three then, but he wouldn't look it for years. The big surprise was that Max was Bingo's lover. There were fifty-nine years between their ages!

The customers started to arrive about eight, and by ten the place was full of laughing and giggling guys. The music grew louder and almost succeeded in drowning out all conversation. I caught glimpses of frantic dancers shaking themselves on the dance floor at the far end of the room. I had never seen such a flock of queens. Max told me to "make" them buy lots of beers. He and I, as well as three other employees, rushed to serve everybody.

"Flirt with 'em," Max whispered, and I tried. One tity-boo was coming on to one man after another, moving up and down the bar, as the guys he approached discouraged him. This fellow had to be at least forty, but even Kei was more mature. The tity-boo started on me.

"Honey, I've never seen you here before!'

"I'm new. First night." I was uncomfortable.

"With that red hair you'll do just fine, doll. What's your name?"

"Strut...it's a nickname. Care for another beer?"

"Sure, why not?" He pushed money toward me. "Gimme a draft."

When I served him and put his change on the bar, he covered my hand with his.

"How about us going to my apartment after the bar closes? I'd like to see you strut your stuff!" He rolled his eyes and laughed at his little joke.

A new group of guys came in and situated themselves farther down the bar. One of them beckoned to me, and I excused myself, moving toward them.

"Knock 'em dead. sweetheart," the queen called out and then moved on to another man.

Because cleanup time was before the bar opened, we bartenders and waiters left after closing, as soon as we cleared the glasses and bottles away. Within a few nights I grew accustomed to The Greene Room and learned to understand the excitement generated by the men and the music.

Once in a while we had lesbian customers who would invariably sit at the tables, rather than stand at the bar. Ninety-nine per cent of the business, though, was male. Some of the guys were masculine, and I was attracted to a few of them. I never did more than flirt and push the beer. On rare occasions hustlers came in, but we discouraged them. They had a difficult time getting our attention to order drinks.

Tony Pogue remained sullen and only spoke to me to give orders, but Max remained kind and friendly. He and I fell into the habit of having coffee and conversation in a corner booth after closings.

Max sincerely loved old Bingo and had mutual sex with him. The two of them lived together upstairs, the younger caring for the older's needs. Gentle Max was a rare bird.

"And that is sufficient for you?" I asked.

"No, I guess it ain't, because I cruise East Ocean View Avenue two or three nights a week." Max poured more cream in his coffee. "Gonna make the run tonight...after I check on Bingo."

"Whom do you pick up? Sailors?"

"Not much. Too risky. Might get beat up or killed, even, messing with them." Max slurped his coffee. "I get hustlers; they don't charge too much, and I got no expenses to speak of, except buying some clothes every now and then. Bingo knows all about it; he don't care."

All I knew about East Ocean View Avenue was that it ran along the Chesapeake Bay and was an odd mixture of expensive homes, decrepit cottages, and honky-tonk bars. The adjective most used to describe it was "sleazy."

"There's both men and women streetwalkers out there. Mostly after all the bars close at two o'clock."

"Are the men attractive?"

"In a way. Most of 'em are burned out. You know, druggies. They'll do anything for money to buy booze or pot or coke. Some are on heroin. You have to hide your wallet before picking one of 'em up. Just have enough money in your pocket to pay 'em."

"I have lived here all my life, and I did not know any of that." I finished my coffee and stood up to go.

"East Ocean View is a place where anybody can make out," Max said. Perhaps he thought I needed the contact.

"It sounds like the Street of Broken Dreams to me."

I left Max laughing. From that night on he referred to East Ocean View Avenue as the Street of Broken Dreams.

Two weeks later, Max and Bingo invited me over early to have supper with them. I hadn't even noticed the kitchen area in one corner of the large upstairs room. When Max had placed the food on the table, he gave Bingo his arm and slowly walked the old man to his chair.

"The ham's delicious, Max. I didn't know you could cook," I complimented him.

"I learned to cook early. My mother was sickly, and somebody had to fix the meals. Now's better, though. Bingo lets me spend a lot more on the groceries."

Max patted Bingo's hand affectionately, and the old man smiled. It was evident that they had a caring relationship, if not a conventional one. Bingo turned his attention to me.

"Max tells me you are a hard worker, Strut. I had a good feeling, a gut feeling about you that first night."

"Thank you, sir."

"Not sir...Bingo. I don't want any Widdicombe saying sir to me. You're the one, boy, with the *blue* blood in your veins!"

"Speaking of colors," I said, "why is the bar named The Greene Room? Does it have to do with the original decor years ago?"

There was suddenly a silence, and Bingo and Max looked at each other. Finally Max spoke.

"You're the first person I ever heard ask that question since I been here. Odd, ain't it? Most people just take the name for granted."

"Hell, don't put him off, Max." Bingo's voice became stronger. "I'll tell him! No need to hide my story from Strut."

I protested. "It wasn't my intention to pry."

"Shut up, boy, and listen." Bingo's eyes became very clear. "Reuben Greene was my lover. We were young, barely in our twenties, when we took up with each other. I was a bartender down on East Main Street, and he was a dock worker. And one hell of a man he was! Strong, strapping man with muscles like a young god. We scraped and saved for years for the money to buy this old barn."

Max rose and went to stand behind Bingo, resting his hands on the old man's frail shoulders.

"Once we bought it, I operated it as a straight bar. It was called "Teddy's." Weren't no dancing here then, and I closed at midnight. After that it was a private club for gay men and women from twelve-thirty 'til two-thirty."

"Only gay place in Norfolk in those days," Max added.

"Reuben and I lived right up here," Bingo continued, "but he never worked in the bar...stayed with his job unloading ships. Loved hard work in the outdoors."

"I wish Reuben *had* left the docks and worked in the bar," Max mumbled. Bingo reached a bony hand up and patted one of Max's hands.

"One day on the docks, a rope or cable or some damn thing hoisting a piano crate broke, and the heavy box landed on Reuben. He was a goner."

All three of us were silent. I was momentarily at a loss for words. Finally I reached over and kissed Bingo on the cheek.

"The next month I changed the name to The Greene Room. Why, your Aunt Charlotte," Bingo brightened, remembering those earlier years, "why, I met her right here...downstairs, I mean. She was a beautiful young woman. And her lover, Lydia Something, she was more what you'd call handsome. A tall sturdy young woman."

Bingo's memory served him well. He could recall Lydia Hooker's first name over all those years, yet he did not know the names of all six of his current employees. Is this what Claire called short-term memory loss?

"Except for my Max here," he said, "the past is more real for me than the present. But I know what's going on around me. I'll always know what's happening."

"Thank you for telling me about Reuben," I said.

Max, living totally in the present, mentioned Tony Pogue's moodiness.

Bingo agreed with his lover's assessment of the manager's personality, but reminded him that Tony was a capable and intelligent manager and, in addition, could handle any straight troublemakers who set foot in the bar.

"But most of the crowd is content to drink, dance, and make out," Max said.

"This is an ongoing learning experience for me," I commented. "So many of the customers seemed to be programmed to find sex partners. Some tity-boos come in night after night, deadly intent on making sexual connections."

"That's right," Max verified.

"And they are immature, acting half their ages," I continued. "Arrested development."

"Suppression," Bingo snapped. "This bar is their refuge. Gay bars are sometimes the *only* place they have to go. To escape a suppressive straight world."

Suddenly I understood. "You are right!" I exclaimed. "We are all outlaws in the Commonwealth of Virginia."

Bingo went on, "And outlaws have to hide, to suppress their true selves...most of the time."

"I must be more sympathetic. Even though I am more protected than they, we are all social outcasts."

The old man was wise; he understood the tity-boos a long time ago. What he had said was as true today as it was sixty years ago.

About a year later I realized that Tony Pogue was stealing a portion of each night's receipts. On two consecutive nights, while I was stacking dirty glasses and discarding beer bottles, I watched him slip some of the nightly take into his jacket pocket. He never knew I observed him.

After the second night I requested a mid-afternoon conference upstairs with Bingo and Max. The result was the firing of Pogue.

Bingo asked me to take over management. I was grateful to him for the expression of trust and glad to get the raise.

My life at the bar opened a new realm for me. Previously I had had no experience with bar life or with the gay community at large. I was learning to mingle with all types of homosexuals.

Charlotte's advice came back to me: "Never be too proud to mingle with the common people. They can be your salvation."

The bar's profits were a disappointment; they were modest. The Greene Room was not the bonanza I had imagined it to be. The waiters and bartenders must sell more beer, but there were other possibilities. Dinners could be offered on weekend evenings. Professional entertainment once a month should draw. I intended to refine my ideas and then present them to Bingo.

Two months later I did. Bingo and I were alone upstairs; he was sitting in an armchair, and I was standing in front of him. Max had gone out for groceries.

"Beer sales are up slightly, Bingo. I intend to increase them even more. Even If I have to put the waiters and bartenders in bikinis." Bingo smiled a toothy grin.

"Than there's the kitchen behind the bar. Except for the refrigerator and the sink, we don't use it at all. Max is a hell of a cook, too." He seemed far away in his own thoughts.

"Are you listening? We could serve food on weekend night, Bingo. Start small with hamburgers and hot dogs." Bingo's eyes looked vacant.

"Then work our way into dinners," I continued. No reason we can't condition the men to come in for dinner *before* drinking. Right now they probably go out somewhere else to eat and come here afterwards."

"Why do you want to make so much more money, Strut?" Bingo asked. "We're doing all right as it is."

"Because if we don't do it, someone else will. Gay guys spend money; let's get our share. And then there are the gay women, the lesbians. I want to attract their business. This is a large building."

Bingo sighed.

"I'm serious about making changes in the bar in order to increase our income."

Bingo nodded his head slowly. "We don't draw many lesbians;

do what you can to attract them, Strut." Bingo sank back into the depths of his chair. "But as for the food line, wait. I'll think about it."

I knew that elderly people were reluctant to accept changes, so I decided to bide my time and approach him later.

During the next year we sought the lesbian business. Starting with a Women's Night on Thursdays, our instructed waiters and bartenders made them welcome in The Greene Room. I learned that a number of our regular male customers already had lesbian friends, and they began bringing them in. Slowly our business became about equally divided between male and female. I liked that.

In April of that year, Bingo died in Max's arms. His body was simply worn out. The old man had refused to be hospitalized; I think he was ready to go.

I comforted Max, insisting he stay at Widdicombe House so he wouldn't be alone. Neil watched over him while I was at work, but he was uncomfortable in the old mansion and asked to return "home" after two days.

Bingo's will left the business to Max and me, jointly. I continued on as manager. Max knew he was not capable of the job.

We began serving dinners a week later, and the take increased. It had been a long overdue step. I chose my most intelligent waiter, Sam Zole, to train to be my assistant manager.

Only a week later I was shocked to see Judith Trilling and another woman sitting at one of our tables in The Greene Room. Had she heard that I managed a gay bar and decided to see for herself? I hesitated, not knowing what to do. Then I decided to face her. Steeling myself. I walked over to her table.

"Strut, I was hoping I'd see you." She greeted me. "Please sit with us."

"For a few minutes, Judith," I answered, seating myself. "Have to stay on top of things here."

"Judy, Strut, not Judith." she said.

She introduced me to the woman with her who was wearing a tailored suit. Her name was Pam Wilburn.

"I had to twist Judy's arm to persuade her to come here tonight." Pam smiled at me. She didn't want to put you on the defensive."

"And now you know without a doubt that I'm gay, Judy. Does it make any difference? Is our friendship terminated?"

"Oh, Strut, hush." She affectionately squeezed my arm. "Coming here was my way...or, our way...of breaking the ice. Do you think I'd be here if I were straight?"

Everything fell into place. Why hadn't I realized this lovely young woman I'd known for years was gay? I mentally reminded myself that I wasn't as intelligent as I had thought. The revelation elated me.

"You should have told me years ago, Judy, back in 1970." I beamed. "You knew about me, certainly. I'm not exactly butch!"

"I didn't know how you'd feel about that," she answered. "I was ready, but I wasn't sure you were. Does Claire know?"

"Yes, but all is unspoken there. She prefers it that way."

I caught a waiter's attention and ordered more beer, telling him there was to be no tab. Then I explained about Vic's dumping me because of Oliver's embezzlement and suicide. Judy had liked Vic.

"He's a fool," Pam interjected. "To a family like the Widdicombes, that's small potatoes."

"I hope so," I responded, "but we are still working our way through it...with Norfolk's upper echelons."

"How *is* Claire?" Judy asked. "She is unique. I glimpse her at church on Sundays. Not you, though, Strut. And I hardly know Keith."

"Kei, he prefers that. Judy, I'm positive he's a member of the club!"

"All right!" cheered Pam.

"Then I want to know him better." Judy smiled. "I'll be over next week...in the late afternoon. Is that convenient?"

"Oh, yes, and bring Pam, I answered.

"Sorry," Pam said, "I'll be working."

*Pam is one of my engineers, and I keep her busy. Business is terrific."

It was becoming late, and the noisy bar needed my attention. Excusing myself, I said I expected to see them both at Saint Paul's Sunday and Judy at Widdicombe House a few days later. Judy's honesty that night pleased me, and I had instantly liked her lover, Pam.

I closed the checkbook for The Greene Room. There were still the household bills to pay. A knock on the library doors from the maid was a welcome interruption.

"Miss Trilling," she announced.

Judy came in and hugged me warmly. I sensed that this feminine woman wanted to be an ally, and I liked that. How did she function in a gay relationship, yet appear heterosexual in the straight business world? She was too successful to be indiscreet in her personal life. After we sat in leather chairs by the front windows, I asked her.

"Strut, it matters less what I do than what people think I do. Right now I am the darling of the real estate developers ...considered bright, pretty, and successful. Yet each year I get more questions about marriage and love and settling down. The women are as nosy as the men."

"Then we can help each other. We can be seen together. Do you think Norfolk will believe I've gone straight if we become an item, Judy?"

"Yes. People usually think we made the choice to be gay, but you and I know it's an 'I am,' not 'I choose.' They'll think you chose to give it up and be 'normal,' without a doubt. And I'd like that, Strut, our being an item, as you put it."

"I will do whatever I can to put the family on solid social and financial ground again, Judy." I excused myself to ask a maid to bring us drinks, and then we resumed our conversation.

"Strut, do you remember what I said to you at your father's funeral?"

"That was three years ago."

"I said that success and gentry, when combined, become powerful. I know that is true."

"And I believe it. However, by the word, combined, do you refer to marriage?"

"It is something to think about. To be honest, though, I couldn't go to bed with a man. I would be ready for Eastern State Hospital in Williamsburg!"

"And I the same for women," I smiled. "Yet children would be a desirable result from such a union."

"Imagine lots of little redheaded Widdicombes running around,

Strut, and two insane parents hovering over them!"

"Yet there must be ways, Judy."

Claire barged in unexpectedly and, after putting down her glass of port, embraced Judy.

"The maid told me you were here, darling," Claire exclaimed. "You're overdue, but I forgive you. Tell me everything you're doing. I keep hearing about your magic touch in real estate."

Judy explained that the first phase of her Trilling Industrial Park was about to open. "There will be manufacturing plants, warehouses, corporate offices, and wholesale outlets. Of course, all my net worth is on paper."

"But someday," I spoke up, "you'll be the top land developer in eastern Virginia. Someday not too distant."

"We are very proud of you, Judy." Claire congratulated her.

"The governor will be here to speak at the official opening." Judy looked at me as she spoke. "It is the same day as the Gilmore-Thayer wedding. Only two hours before, as a matter of fact."

"Claire and I will have no trouble being at the grand opening," I said. "We are not invited to the wedding."

Judy was speechless.

"I prefer to be at the Industrial park's opening anyway." Claire smiled. It is still Governor Catching, isn't it? I mean they haven't elected another one yet, have they?"

"Still Governor Catching," Judy answered.

"I grew up with him...haven't seen him since the thirties," Claire mused. "His family moved to Petersburg back then."

Judy and I eyed each other. We were both having the same idea. I grinned, and she laughed aloud.

"Claire, you have been remiss in your social obligations these past several years." I took her hand as I talked. "It would be downright rude of you to neglect the governor while he is here."

"Why, I guess it would...." She looked puzzled.

"You are going to have a reception for Governor Catching and his wife—"

"At the same time as the Gilmore-Thayer wedding," Judy finished.

"My, what a splendid idea," Claire cried out. "I'm only upset that I did not think of it myself! I'll phone the man today."

"I don't want to sound *nouveau riche*," Judy added, "but spare no expense. I'll pick up all the bills, and I insist on that."

Three weeks later Trilling Industrial Park opened with fanfare. The governor addressed the throng of developers, merchants, and other interested persons. When he was finished, he moved back to his seat. It was between his wife, Maude, and his old friend, Claire. Judy was seated on the other side of Maude.

An hour later the four of them were in the receiving line at Widdicombe House with Kei and me. As the guests passed through the line, Neil, Pam Wilburn, and Jessie Cobb invited them into the formal dining room for refreshments.

The house glittered almost blatantly. The June weather was perfect, and all the downstairs windows were open. Three maids took charge of the light wraps. Extra servants had been employed, and waiters moved smoothly from the kitchen, where Mrs. O'Brian was in charge of the food and beverages. Silver trays holding glasses of French champagne were carried throughout the drawing room, as well as the music room, where a string quartet played. An abundance of freshly cut flowers brightened the rooms and the vestibule. The large crystal chandeliers sparkled overhead, and the congenial voices of impressed and affable guests mingled.

When all the guests had arrived, the receiving line dissolved. Maude Catching stayed close to Claire, enjoying the old glory of the Widdicombe's entertaining in their ancestral home. Claire was radiant in a grey gown with her diamond necklace and matching bracelet, family pieces.

Kei gravitated to Bradley Boddicker who was standing beside his grandparents. They were engaging wealthy Derrick Agnew in conversation.

Agnew was a startlingly attractive man, thirty-five years old, with blue eyes and prematurely silver-grey hair. He lived in fine style on tobacco money. The man was connected to powerful families in Durham and Winston-Salem, North Carolina.

I approached this group and joined in the conversation. Mrs. Boddicker said that if Bradley continued staying at Widdicombe House so frequently, she should pay us room and board. Everyone laughed, and Derrick Agnew scrutinized the boys.

"Gentlemen, the stronger drinks are in the family dining room,"

I told Agnew and Mr. Boddicker. "If you are so inclined, please indulge yourselves."

"Mister Widdicombe, seeing Keith here this evening causes me to wonder about his brothers. Are they also present?" Agnew asked me.

"We cast out the bad apples," I answered. "They live out of town somewhere." I smiled and excused myself, but Agnew took hold of my arm. The Boddickers and Kei moved away.

"May I have a few words with you privately?" Agnew looked intent.

"We can talk in the library," I responded, ushering him toward that room, "but only for a few moments. I don't want to be criticized for being an absent host."

After I turned on a table lamp and closed the sliding doors, I turned to face my guest. The man was attractive in an unusual way. His Roman nose and strong features were sensual, and there was the promise of a well-built frame under the tailor-made dinner jacket.

"First, young man. I want to congratulate you. You have saved a sinking ship...and put it back on course. I admire that."

"Thank you. I did what I had to do."

"Even to working in, er, managing a gay bar. I know all about that."

"Being an employee there doesn't necessarily mean I am...homosexual." I took a step backwards, but he advanced.

"And I desire you, young Strutwick."

The man caught me in his arms and pressed his mouth to mine. I tried to resist, but his strong arms were a vise. His lips forced mine open; his tongue probed inside my mouth. I did not yield to him until his grip hurt me. Stirred, I began to return his hard wet kisses. When we separated, we were both panting. I moved toward the doors.

"This isn't right," I said. "We will forget it happened and not speak of it, Mr. Agnew."

"Derrick!...call me Derrick, Strutwick."

I opened the doors and left him there. Mingling among the guests, I saw his wife, Natalie Agnew. She was looking for him.

Claire left the people with whom she had been talking and

pulled me aside. "Jessie has taken Maude Catching under her wing, for the time being," Claire said. "Find Judy, dear, and make sure she meets the people she doesn't already know."

"I will, and you may think of Judy and me as a couple. The Widdicombes shall not live lives of genteel poverty," I whispered in her ear.

She laughed and then pulled my head close to her mouth. "The Widdicombes are a curious breed."

We both smiled and then moved in different directions. I found Judy talking to the governor. He thanked me profusely for the reception in his honor.

When we were able, Judy and I slipped away and went into the family dining room. Neil and Pam were informally hosting and conversing with a group of professional and business men. A fellow engineer was taken with Pam, and she feigned interest nicely. I was proud of her. The busy bartender looked at Judy and smiled. Judy had "stolen" him from the Botetourt Yacht and Country Club, scene of Vic Gilmore's wedding reception.

I kissed Judy on the cheek and then went into the kitchen. Mrs. O'Brian was presiding over the activity there in fine form.

"You are a wonder," I said, going over and kissing her, too.

"It's Miss Claire's doings, not mine. She organized it all, from A to Z. What's bred in the bone is born in the flesh. Just comes natural to her."

I hugged her and went to the telephone and dialed. At The Greene Room, Sam Zole reported all was well there. I promised to be in before he closed at two in the morning. When I hung up, I started out the door.

"You look like a million dollars in your dinner jacket, Mister Strutwick," Mrs. O'Brian called after me. I turned and winked.

In the meantime, I could see Derrick and Natalie Agnew leaving through the front door. I was relieved. Rejoining Judy, we circulated until some of the other guests started to go. Claire and the Catchings. had stationed themselves by the leaded glass front door, so Judy and I moved that way.

In forty minutes the rest of the guests were gone. The governor and his wife thanked us again and they left in his limousine. Only Jessie Cobb remained, and we had insisted earlier that she stay and join us for our little family supper.

I did not see Kei or Bradley, who was spending the night, anywhere. When it was time to sit down for our meal, Neil and I went in search of the boys. While Neil checked the house, I went outside and into the walled garden. All was quiet there, and I momentarily inhaled the fragrance of the garden.

Then I heard a soft sound. Walking toward the gazebo, I inadvertently surprised the boys. Bradley was locked in Kei's arms, and they were kissing passionately.

CHAPTER SEVEN

"Not here, Kei!" I rushed to the boys. Startled, they broke from their embrace and stared at me. Bradley looked terrified. "You could be seen! Both of you are being reckless!"

Bradley began to cry and put his hands over his face. I sat on the wooden seat in the gazebo, clasping the boy close to me and encircling him with one arm. Embarrassed, Kei sat down on the other side of me.

"I didn't intend to frighten you, Bradley, but you boys shocked me."

"I'm sorry, Mister Widdicombe! Really I am!"

Bradley's sobs subsided as I soothed him and stroked his hair. He calmed down and wiped his eyes with my handkerchief.

"Please realize, Bradley, that I am not being critical. I merely insist you and Kei use discretion. Many people, having seen you kissing, would find it a repugnant sight."

"I understand, Strut," Kei said, leaning against me. "Suppose Claire had seen us, or Mrs. O'Brian!"

"That's the point." I smiled at my nephew and put my other arm around him. "Most of the western world today does not accept homosexual love. People can become hostile. They can spread vicious gossip, damage reputations, wound families."

"We'll be careful." Bradley nodded. "As long as you aren't mad with me...uh, us."

"Not at all. In fact I give you boys my blessing and my support," I affectionately hugged them. "At your age I never had that from anybody. Now come inside for dinner. The others are waiting."

"Yes, sir!" Bradley smiled.

"And, Kei, take Bradley to wash his face before coming to table. You can enter privately through my bedroom...and a stolen kiss in the powder room is acceptable!"

I returned to the family dining room before the boys arrived and covered for them by saying we had gotten caught up in a personal conversation.

"Oh, a father-son talk?" Claire raised her eyebrows.

"Sometimes it takes a lot of doing to get this family all together!" Mrs. O'Brian cast a severe look at me. "Won't have my veal cooling off before you all get to the table."

She put down the steaming platter and went to the kitchen to fetch salad and bread. When the boys came in, Kei took his seat next to me, and Bradley slipped into the chair next to Kei.

"I'm eager to get a headcount on the guests at the Gilmore-Thayer reception," Judy said.

"My dear, I'll have that for us in a day or so," Jessie assured her. "It's information I can pick up. Marjorie Thayer's great aunt will most likely volunteer it."

"Your diamonds take my breath away, Mrs. Widdicombe." Pam admired Claire's necklace and bracelet. "They must be family pieces."

"Thank you, dear. They are. But do try to call me Claire. Surnames are a nuisance among friends."

"Claire's probably stockpiling all the Widdicombe family jewelry until she has a daughter-in-law," Jessie commented.

"Or a grand-daughter-in-law." Claire glanced at Kei and smiled. "When Kei marries, I shall bejewel his bride admirably."

Kei's smile vanished, and he cast a suppliant look at me. I remained silent in order to assess his reaction. At this point, however, I did not discern Kei as the future Widdicombe stud unless Bradley could somehow mysteriously conceive.

"And the crowning pieces are Carolyn's ruby choker and earrings!" Claire added.

"I think I'm going to be a bachelor...like Strut!" Kei protested.

"When you are older, dear, you will feel differently about marriage." Claire spoke sweetly. "The love of a good woman is part of your destiny."

"May I apply early?" Pam interjected on seeing Kei's discomfort. "I'm available and willing to wait!"

Everyone laughed, and I changed the subject to Trilling Industrial Park. Judy cooperated and explained her plans for the future, which included a shopping mall.

On Sunday we attended Saint Paul's en masse, causing a turning of heads and a whispering of comments throughout the congregation. The seating order in our pew was Jessie, Claire, Kei, Judy, myself, Neil, and Pam. After service our entire party was deluged by friendly parishioners. I remembered what Judy had said about the combination of success and gentry. I think our greeters sniffed the possibility of such a merger.

That afternoon I was alone in the library, typing up scattered old Widdicombe notes for the journal, when Mrs. O'Brian briefly poked her head in the door to tell me to pick up the phone. I was startled to hear Vic Gilmore's voice.

"You win, Strut. Guess I was wrong."

It had been years since I had heard his deep voice, and its vibrant quality still seduced me. I was provoked with myself for this weakness.

"Whatever do you mean, Vic?"

"I mean that my wedding was a social disaster because I ran up against you."

"I am not aware that you...ran up against me, as you put it."

"Marjorie and I had only our families and some company employees at our wedding and reception!"

"Blame me if you wish, but I did not set the date for the dedication of Trilling Industrial Park. Is your anger due to Claire's reception for the governor? He is an old friend of hers."

"No, I'm trying to say that I was wrong, Strut. Wrong not to invite you and Claire to my wedding."

"Is it possible you believe we would have attended? I'm not a masochist, Vic."

"Oh, damn it all, Strut, I'm a fool! I shouldn't have deserted you!"

"I needed you when Oliver shot himself...needed your love and support so much, but you turned from me. Humiliated, weren't you? Didn't you know that this house, the house of Widdicombe, would prevail?"

"I love you, Strut."

"Don't say that! Never say that to me again!"

"Let me see you. I'll come over right now! Just say I can!"

"Those are strange words coming from a bridegroom!"

"You know I don't love Marjorie! My mother arranged that ...pushed me into it!"

"It is late, and I must leave for The Greene Room."

"You, running a gay bar! I've heard it, but I still can't believe it."

"Believe! Even the Widdicombes have to eat, Vic. I'd rather be low class than middle class! No men's haberdashery for me, thank you!"

"Everybody in Norfolk is talking about you tending bar!"

"*Was* talking about it. It never came up at the governor's reception! Nevertheless, I prefer to be regarded as notorious rather than as ordinary."

"Can't we meet secretly?"

"And behave like trash? I don't think my lover would take kindly to such tryst. Now, I must go, Vic. Don't call me again. That's beating a dead horse."

Once I hung up, I crumpled, putting my head down on the large desk. Although dry-eyed, I agonized. The longing for Vic Gilmore was still a part of me, but a second telephone call jolted me back to the present.

"Strutwick, this is Derrick Agnew. I want to see you tonight!" The voice was assertive. "We can have dinner together."

The tobacco heir with his iron embrace. He was pursuing me, and I didn't intend to allow it to continue.

"Don't you think your wife would object to that, Mr. Agnew? Wouldn't she resent your attention to me?"

"To hell with Natalie! It's you I desire! See me tonight. I'll demonstrate how good a lover I am."

"Lusty words!"

"I am very good at what I do!"

"And I do not doubt you. Mr. Agnew, you are a fine catch, but I am not interested, and I must leave for The Greene Room. I should already be there."

Hanging up, I hurriedly put away the family notes and journals and then left for the bar. My love-hate feelings for Vic were still very vivid; I had to hold my emotions in check. And as for the wealthy Derrick Agnew, with cold blue eyes and silvergrey hair, Jessie Cobb had once said he was as flamboyant as the *nouveau riche*, but that his family truly was old southern aristocracy. He did not behave so with me. I felt confused when he talked to me, experiencing a feeling akin to struggling in quicksand. Best to keep the door barred against him.

Days ran into months and months into years. The Widdicombes were living well, but neither Neil nor I could put any funds aside. I was so busy managing the bar and providing for my family that I postponed discussing marriage further with Judy. Even so, she and Pam visited Widdicombe House often.

By 1976 Claire was fretting over church affairs. At sixty-one she wasn't receptive to the proposed changes in the prayer book or to the possibility of the church's admitting women to the priesthood. "Times are changing," she had said, "but I prefer life the way it was. Women priests, imagine! Do you think they will wear trousers? It simply isn't fitting!"

Jessie Cobb had turned seventy-nine, but the remarkable woman refused to yield to old age. Sweet Max, my co-heir to The Greene Room, still lived upstairs in the bar and assisted me with many of the errands for the business. Although twenty-nine, no one would have thought him to be over twenty-one. He took no serious interest in any man and continued to cruise the Street of Broken Dreams. Neil Rice remained devoted to me and loyal to my family. I wished I was able to love him more than I did.

Kei at seventeen was a handsome young man, his big brown eyes and darkening red hair complimented by a sturdy body and a masculine demeanor. A senior at Maury High School, he was a bonafide football star. Moreover, he was still in love with Bradley Boddicker who was a senior at the prestigious Calvert school for Boys, and almost too pretty for a boy.

My primary concern was how I would be able to afford to send Kei to Washington and Lee University. That, and the severe need for a new roof on The Greene Room, caused me grave vexation.

On a Sunday afternoon I was in my bedroom downstairs when Kei knocked and entered. He, Bradley, Judy, and Pam had just returned from a weekend shopping trip to Richmond, and I had known that Judy paid for the overnight trip's expenses. He hugged and kissed me affectionately.

"Guess what Mrs. O'Brian just said to me, Strut."

"I've no idea. She sees herself as the mother hen of us all and is capable of uttering any choice thought that enters her head."

I rested a hand on my china clock while I admired Kei. He was already taller than I was and magnificently built. I allowed myself to feel pride in the young man.

"She told me that she hoped I didn't have rooster blood in my veins like great grandfather Cedric Widdicombe because I sure was beginning to look like him!"

We laughed about Mrs. O'Brian's observation. From photographs of my grandfather that I remembered seeing, I decided she was correct as to the resemblance.

"Oh, and there's more news, Strut." Kei's eyes brightened. "Something I think will make you happy."

"I am happy," I said, running a finger over the graceful curves of the china clock. I had yet to take it out for repair, but I loved the beautiful old timepiece.

"Happier then." Kei grinned. "Your frustrated pursuer has gone to Rome!"

"What are you trying to say?"

"Derrick Agnew! Remember, the man of a thousand phone calls? He's divorcing his wife! Sent her back to Atlanta, where she's from, and went to live it up in Rome. Guess he'll find some, ah—"

"Diversion? Yes, Rome could provide that. I hope he will find someone permanent in Italy."

"Bradley heard it from his father. It seems Agnew's sexual interests are fairly well known around town."

"My heart grows fond of his absence." I misquoted. "Thank you for bearing such welcome news."

Again I looked at my old clock. First Oliver had procrastinated in taking it out for repairs, and now I had. "Think you can find a box to place this in, Kei? It goes to a clock repair shop tomorrow."

It was heavy, and I tilted it as I picked it up. The brass door on it's backside flew open.

"Oops!" I exclaimed, trying to level it.

"What's that?" Kei exclaimed, coming to my side.

We laid it face down on the bed, its brass doorplate askew.

"My god, it's Oliver's money!" I cried, pulling out a fistful of one hundred dollar bills.

Kei and I emptied the clock. It had been stuffed with bills in fifty and one hundred dollar denominations.

"Oliver hid the embezzled money in the clock! Probably a little at a time, Strut!"

We flattened out the money and counted it. Two hundred fifteen thousand dollars had been stuffed into the antique clock. It was no wonder the piece did not keep time.

"It's difficult to believe that this money was right here in my bedroom through all the years we lived on the brink of bankruptcy! Kei, your college tuition is here." I felt that burden lift from my shoulders. "The new roof for The Greene Room, too! The rest can go into certificates of deposit or some other sound investments."

Kei looked at me in surprise.

"Strut, we have to give it to the bank. To keep it would be stealing."

"No! We need it! Have you forgotten the shame and scandal we endured? We've earned this money!"

"Sure, we suffered because of Oliver's stealing it." He put his arm around my shoulders. "You, especially. You lost Vic Gilmore and had to go to work tending bar. But we still have to return the money. It's the bank's. Remember, we are Widdicombes, and, no matter what, we have to keep our self-respect." Kei was uncompromising.

When the money was returned, Kei and I consented to be interviewed by the Virginian-Pilot. Once the feature story was printed, we were stopped by people everywhere and praised. For a time the Widdicombes were the city's heros. All the public acknowledgment of our honesty did not put a penny in our pockets.

Before the year was out, I got wind that out-of-town money was opening a new bar and disco in Norfolk. It would hurt business at The Greene Room, which was in need of a new roof. I also heard that Derrick Agnew had returned from Rome and hoped he would keep his distance.

In early 1977 the new bar opened and began bringing in live entertainment on weekends. Our business suffered. Agnew came in The Greene Room several times and tried to start conversations with me; I was genuinely too busy to talk because we had cut our staff to less than half. Even Neil helped out on weekend nights, working gratis.

Once the excitement over the glitzy new bar subsided, we

regained some of our lost customers, but business was still less than it had been. By the time Kei left for Lexington to start his first semester at Washington and Lee, I had scraped up only one year's tuition. I mailed the school a check for the entire year while I still had the money.

In November Pam and Judy drove up to spend the weekend with Kei, picking up Bradley, a University of Richmond freshman, on the way. The four of them would attend a football game and enjoy their reunion.

It seemed to me that it had rained so much already that month, but on the Saturday night of that weekend the rain was hard and unrelenting. The understaffed Greene Room was busier than usual, and Derrick Agnew sat at the bar drinking beer and watching me rush about.

Suddenly a portion of the roof in one area began to leak badly. Customers jumped in, helping to move tables, and Sam Zole and I began to mop frantically. The water was coming in as fast as we filled our buckets until mercifully the deluge ended. A few minutes later I sat down in the back booth to drink a cup of coffee and calm my nerves. Seemingly from nowhere, Derrick Agnew slid in beside me and put his beer on the table.

"Rotten luck, Strutwick."

"I knew it would happen one day...or one night, as it is. The roof has been ready to go for some time now." Too exhausted to be aloof, I conversed with the man, noticing his arms bulging from his expensive short-sleeve sport shirt. "No funds, Mr. Agnew. We have to live with this old roof."

"Call me Derrick, Strutwick." He reminded me impatiently. "If you hadn't avoided me all this time, your damned roof wouldn't be caving in now! I can help."

He pressed his leg against mine, and I could feel his body heat. He smiled, white teeth flashing from a perfectly tanned face. The man exuded an animal-like sensuality.

"You do know Neil Rice is my lover?"

"Rice is a wimp who can't help you, Strutwick."

"He is kind and honest and—"

"—and of no fucking consequence!" he finished for me. "Furthermore, you do not love him. Are you afraid of a real man?"

He put one powerful arm around my shoulders and pulled me closer. "You know I've wanted you for four years, and I have never waited that long for anybody! Come home with me tonight, when the bar closes."

"I can't," I hesitated, "but I will meet you tomorrow."

"I can wait, but don't stand me up, Widdicombe!" He rubbed his knuckles across my cheek.

Max approached the booth, and my attention was diverted. He told me that his living quarters had been soaked, and I leaped up to try to help him. Several of the bartenders stayed to assist us after The Greene Room closed.

I am not sure *why* I capitulated to Derrick Agnew. I suppose it was the never-ending struggle for money. Perhaps it was the lack of excitement in my relationship with Neil. Although it had had a promising beginning, Neil was not interesting at all in bed, and our sexual activity had become mechanical.

For whatever the reasons, I went to Agnew's condominium at two o'clock the next afternoon. He lived in a new high rise, and his apartment was on the top floor. Riding the elevator, I was impressed with all the chrome and steel. When I stepped into the hall, I noticed that there was a service elevator, too. Convenient. The owners would never have to rub shoulders with delivery people and servants.

I rang and Derrick swung the door open wide. He was wearing only a short robe, and I was fascinated by his strong muscular legs. I walked in, and, closing the door behind me, he followed me into the luxurious living room. He was barefoot.

"When you walk out of here, Strutwick, you won't be the same man."

"Have you lived here long?" I asked, trying to make small talk.

"Bought the condo when I returned from Rome." He put a hairy arm around me and led me onto the balcony. "While I was gone, my house was sold. Now how's that for a view? Great, huh?" Derrick waved his free hand, and I looked out over downtown Norfolk and the Elizabeth River.

I was uneasy, and, when I gazed into his hard blue eyes, he must have sensed it. His thick silver-grey hair was being windblown, and I felt an urge to touch it.

"Too cold out here." He guided me back inside and shut the glass door. "I didn't see one man in Rome with dark red hair like yours." He ran his broad hand through it.

"I am not at all sure we should be this familiar." I tried to speak firmly, taking a step backwards.

He pulled me to him and reached inside my shirt, popping a button. His hand moved roughly over my pectorals. When he squeezed one, my mouth flew open, but he kissed me hard, swallowing my groan.

"It's high time you learned what passion is about, Strutwick!" He locked my body against his. "If I have to drag you to my bed, by god, I will! Today I'll teach you how to separate the men from the boys!"

CHAPTER EIGHT

Three days later I was eating a late breakfast alone and wondering why Derrick Agnew hadn't phoned. Was it possible he had wanted me for only a one-night sex-romp? If that were so, then why did he loan me money?

I had left the condominium with his check for a sizable amount. Even though he had drawn up a handwritten promissory note and I had signed it, the loan was at no interest and not due for five years. Had he wished, Derrick could have extracted much more favorable terms from me.

Roofing contractors were to begin tomorrow. I had moved quickly to commence the work. In addition I had borrowed sufficient money to add an office and a stage to The Greene Room. Derrick hadn't limited the amount of the loan; he had helped me to estimate amply the costs of the construction I wanted.

I was still suffering the loss of the money Kei and I had discovered in the china clock. I remembered Charlotte having once said, "There are givers, and there are takers in this world. Which will you be?" It may seem strange, but I think I disappointed her in returning the embezzled funds. There would be no repayment of a loan had I retained Oliver's nest egg.

A smile wreathed my face as I remembered having told Vic Gilmore I wouldn't meet him because it would be behaving like trash. Indeed, I had behaved like trash with Derrick Agnew, and it was the most exciting sexual experience I had ever had.

I still had red welts and some small bruises. He had been a tiger, biting and tearing as we had half-wrestled in his bedroom. It had been lusty abandonment to passionate stimulations and rough orgasms, providing the most completely fulfilling event of my life. Now I wanted more. Hurrying through the rest of my breakfast, I closed myself up in the library and dialed Derrick's number.

"I"ve been expecting your call, Strutwick. What took you so long?"

"I don't exactly know." I was confused by his egotism. "I don't want to make a nuisance of myself."

"Oh? I never have perceived you to be the shy type."

"Be that as it may, I thought I'd drop by to see you before going to The Greene Room."

"Certainly, if your wounds are sufficiently healed. Kiss Neil goodbye and get over here. I'm ready for round two!"

"Derrick, don't joke about Neil. He is not to know about us."

"Screw Neil Rice—and I'll wager I could, too!"

"Have some consideration for the man. He has never said one unkind word about you."

"For right now, I'll keep silent, but I'm not a patient man, Strutwick. Now get over here if it's raw sex you want. And I know you want it!"

In five minutes I was backing the Mercedes out of the carriage house. Knowing Derrick could not be dominated, I decided to be more indirect in dealing with him. Perhaps I could exert more influence over him by taking a subtle approach. During the next two weeks we met eleven times, and I almost missed the grand opening of Trilling Mall, Judy's latest accomplishment.

On a Sunday morning in mid-December, she and Kei startled Claire and me by announcing their engagement.

"Oh, I always assumed you and Strut would marry, Judy." Claire was stunned.

"Kei's only eighteen, Judy, and you and I are twenty-seven. There's such an age gap."

"I'll be nineteen by the time we marry in June." Kei responded.

"Even with the age difference we are compatible." Judy was politely firm.

"Ah, a June bride!" Claire squeezed Judy's hand. "You did surprise me, dear, but I give you both my blessing. Strut is, I'm afraid, wed to that club he manages."

"Maybe it is better this way." I wanted to ask questions, questions that could not be asked in Claire's presence. "I'll always love you both."

"Thank you, Strut." Judy hugged me.

"To think there may be a baby in the house in a year and a half. Marvelous!"

"Not that soon, Claire," Judy answered. "1 think we all want

Kei to finish college. I intend to pay the expenses for the remaining three years at Washington and Lee. It would be the appropriate thing to do. After that we'll talk babies."

Sitting there I felt the burden of paying tuition lift from my shoulders.

Now The Greene Room had a chance to rival the newer bar's competition. Without having to pay Kei's college expenses, I could reinvest in the business.

I was relieved that Kei, not I, would be marrying Judy. I wanted no additional social obligations and intended to spend my leisure time in Derrick's iron embrace. I was obsessed with the man.

Two hours later I was at my desk in the library working on the family journals when Kei slipped in. He closed the sliding doors behind him.

"Always working, aren't you, Strut?"

"Became a habit, I guess." I closed the journals and stacked them. "I want to ask you more about this proposed marriage."

"Guess I should have talked to you first...before Judy and I made it definite to Claire."

"No, no, I approve of it, Kei. Don't be concerned. My personal life is in a state of flux right now. It is better for you, not me, to marry Judy. But I do want to ask a question or two."

"Ask anything, Strut." Kei fidgeted with his tie.

"Are you and Judy planning to have children later, to carry on the Widdicombe name? And, if so, can you manage the bedroom activities?"

"Yes, children...after I finish school. We intend to use artificial insemination. Have it done in Washington, D. C. Can't take the chance of word getting out here in Norfolk."

"Astute reasoning, Kei." I rose and walked to the mantle, resting my arm on it. "And Pam and Bradley? What of them?"

"Judy and I intend to move them in after the wedding. There are enough bedrooms."

"A full house, a poker player might say. Perhaps I am the joker!"

"Don't say that, Strut." Kei looked forlorn. "The family revolves around you. You are at its center."

"Not for much longer. I will allocate that position to you as soon as you are married. You have been groomed for it, and I wish to pursue my personal life."

"I'm not sure I'm—"

"With Judy's help you'll be most satisfactory. As for Claire, I'll help you there, preparing her for the time when Pam and Bradley move into Widdicombe House."

"Do you think Claire knows about all of us, Strut?"

"She does and she doesn't. As long as her objectives are met, she most likely will refuse to acknowledge to herself the homosexual aspects of her family."

"Her objectives?" Kei moved to the window and looked out. "I'm sorry. It's just that Bradley is due over."

"Claire's only goals are to live well, which she will be doing with Trilling money, and to perpetuate the family lineage."

"Oh." Kei saw Bradley's car stop outside. "Judy has already told me that she intends to take over the house expenses."

"That's practically understood," I said, studying his face. "There's another matter, too, Kei. I'm going to need your cooperation."

"Sure. You have it."

"I am seeing Derrick Agnew now, and I don't want Neil to find out."

Kei looked sick and, finding a chair, collapsed into it.

"But why?" He managed to sputter.

"Because I have to have him. Derrick is more exciting than either Neil or Vic."

"Damn! I don't want Neil to know, either."

"Tell only Bradley. Now go to him and put my situation out of your mind. I heard his car stop outside a few moments ago."

Driving over to Derrick's condominium, I thought about the conversation with Kei, and, in particular, my reference to Vic. It had been the first time since becoming intimate with Derrick that Vic had crossed my mind. Incredibly, he did not matter anymore. My former attachment to him seemed now to have been only a youthful fantasy-romance. There was no more yearning for or resentment of Vic. There was nothing at all.

I divided my time between home, Derrick's place, and the bar. I did, however, depend more and more on Sam Zole, my capable assistant manager, to supervise the operation of The Greene Room. After work Neil would occasionally slip downstairs to my bedroom,

HOUSE OF BROKEN DREAMS

and I did not deny him sex.

By February of 1978 Derrick and I were dining in public together. It was reckless, but I did not care. We became the leading topic of gossip in Norfolk. I was concerned that Neil would find out. Even though I was neglecting him, I was reluctant to hurt him. Derrick constantly urged me to tell him and move him out of Widdicombe House.

Neil's small accounting firm increased its business somewhat, but his connection to me hindered its growth. I was still considered outrageous in commercial quarters. Most of the merchants knew that The Greene Room was a gay establishment. Kitty Wenzel was gone, but her malice still touched us. On the positive side, Neil did have a lot of the gay community's business.

In May the newer bar and disco closed, and The Greene Room welcomed an increase in business. The out-of-town bars evidently hadn't found their Norfolk location sufficiently profitable. I started repaying the loan Derrick had made to me.

Also, I was laying the groundwork with Claire for Pam and Bradley to move into the house. As the June wedding date approached, there were plans to be made, and Pam and Bradley were included in the decision-making. They often chauffeured Claire on her errands in preparation for the event. With Judy's mother in California, Claire had eagerly stepped forward to organize the affair. Judy directed her to spare no expense. Frequently Kei and I encouraged Judy, Pam, and Bradley to spend the night. The two unoccupied bedrooms became unofficially assigned to them.

The June wedding at Saint Paul's was simple but beautiful. Judy's only attendant was Pam, and I was Kei's best man. Neil and Bradley were groomsmen. Claire's reception at Widdicombe House exceeded in brilliance her reception for Governor Catching years ago. Vic and Marjorie Gilmore, as well as Derrick Agnew, were among the three hundred guests from Virginia and North Carolina.

Judy and Kei had a short honeymoon in Paris, with Pam and Bradley simultaneously vacationing in Madrid. Of course the four of them came together once they arrived in Europe.

When everyone had returned to Norfolk, life at Widdicombe House settled into a comfortable pattern. It was Claire herself who encouraged Pam and Bradley to live with us. She had grown to love and to depend upon them.

As the years passed, Derrick became the most important person in my life. Behind my back he confronted Neil. Once he had confirmed with me my relationship with Derrick, Neil moved out.

"Neil, I'm sorry it has come to this."

We were in his bedroom, and I was watching him pack his luggage. He would not look me in the face.

"From what Agnew said, everyone in town knew about your affair except me. I can't understand why you kept on having sex with me."

"Because I do care about you, Neil. And I didn't want to hurt you. I still don't."

"Do you love him?"

"I...I don't know. He's dynamic and sensual and forceful, but I don't know if I am in love with him." I slumped to a chair, depressed.

"Maybe you'd best find that out for yourself."

"I'm not sure what love is anymore. Sometimes I think my heart is dead."

"Then I feel sorry for you." Neil looked into my eyes for the first time. Tears were welling in his. "Love, deep love, isn't so easy to find...for straight *or* gay people."

He snapped shut the suitcases and picked them up. "Don't follow me out. This is tough enough as it is."

Then Neil was gone. Within two months he left Norfolk, accepting a position with a large accounting firm in Alexandria. I suffered remorse in having treated him so shabbily and sensed resentment from Kei and Judy.

By January my social life was separate from that of the others. Claire at sixty-six usually retired first and was apparently oblivious to the night traffic between bedrooms on the second floor. Derrick often came to me in my first floor bedroom. Kei and Judy did not accept him and remained cool whenever in his presence.

Judy, Kei, and I were having Saturday lunch in the family dining room one day when Claire burst in. She was bringing us her latest bit of news.

"Jessie Cobb has inherited a beach cottage in Florida. From a widowed cousin, I think."

"Where in Florida?" Kei asked.

"Fort Lauderdale, and she would like to go down and see it. Jessie knows it's waterfront property, and I think she's considering a possible move there...for the winters only, of course."

"The woman's incredible. She will never slow down," Judy smiled.

"I would like to make the trip with her, Strut, if you can manage the expense."

"I will manage it, Claire. You plan on going. In fact, you both should fly."

"Marvelous. Jessie and I, a scouting party of sorts!" Claire exclaimed. "Why, it would almost be an adventure!"

Eagerly anticipating the trip, Claire became as giddy as a school girl. I realized that she had had little opportunity to travel in her life after marrying Oliver. The day before the scheduled flight departure from D.C., I was helping Pam load luggage. She had volunteered to drive the older ladies to Washington, all three intending to spend the night there in a hotel.

"Think my station wagon will hold all their suitcases?" she asked me as we carried them outside. Claire and Mrs. O'Brian were at our heels.

"Do you know I've never flown before?" Claire told Pam. "Is it truly safe?"

"Safer than the highways these days." Pam was reassuring. "And so fast."

"Oh, Mrs. O'Brian, did you put the port in my overnight case?" Claire asked the sixty-six year old housekeeper. "In a thermos?"

"I've done everything you said," Mrs. O' Brian responded. "Lord knows, there's no rest for the weary, and the righteous don't need it! You just concentrate on having a good time, Miss Claire. I'll tend to the rest of this family."

"You won't recognize me when I come home." Claire teased her. "I'll be so suntanned."

"Claire, are you carrying a bathing suit?" I could not imagine her wearing one.

"Heavens, no. I'll not go that far...even in Fort Lauderdale!"

Then Claire and Pam left to pick up Jessie. Mrs. O'Brian and I went into the house smiling.

"This is a big occasion for Claire," I said. "She"s traveled so little."

"Miss Claire out of Widdicombe House!" Mrs. O'Brian rolled her eyes. "Something like this happens only once in a blue moon."

"But take note that she's staying south of the Mason-Dixon line!"

The next day I was at Derrick's. It was after sex, and I was lying on a sofa with my head in his lap. He was trying to persuade me to move into his condominium.

"I love it here, but I have lived in Widdicombe House all my life, Derrick. I can't leave it."

"Then I'll move there...with you. If you love me, you'll live with me, one place or the other."

The phone rang, and Derrick reached for it. I was grateful it had diverted his attention. I could not move him into our home, our lives. Judy and Kei would not tolerate his living there. Moreover, he would be too careless in Claire and Mrs. O'Brian's presence. Derrick's legs tensed, and I gazed up at him.

"Oh, hell! This is going to wreck him! What can I do? ... Yes, I'll have him over there right away!"

"Sounds serious," I said, sitting up, "What was it all about?"

"Get a hold of yourself, Strutwick! This is bad news!" His cold blue eyes stared into mine. "That was your nephew on the phone. This is going to hurt bad!"

"What's happened?" My mouth went dry,

"The plane that your mother and Miss Cobb boarded...Air Florida...crashed into the Potomac River right after take-off! They're gone, both of them, along with lots of other passengers!"

I did not cry, but I began to shake violently. Derrick put his arms around me and held me. I tried to speak but could not. Poor Claire. Her life over in a ringing of a phone! My world would never be the same again. Claire had been my anchor; I never knew it until she was dead.

CHAPTER NINE

"Exactly what is it you wish to discuss?" Judy was cool as she spoke to Derrick Agnew. She would not pretend to like the man.

"I'd like to discuss living with Strutwick. In this house."

"Strut has never mentioned that possibility to us, Mister Agnew," Kei said.

It was eleven p.m. on a July Saturday night in 1988. Kei and Judy had returned home from the Botetourt Yacht and Country Club to find Derrick waiting for them. Despite the nine-year age difference Kei and Judy made a handsome couple. Kei was jaunty and well-formed in his tailored dinner jacket, and Judy sparkled in a low-cut dress of dark blue velvet, adorned by Carolyn's ruby choker and earrings.

A feeling of hostility permeated the drawing room. Kei and Judy disliked the visitor's blunt manners and open defiance of convention. Derrick eyed the strange couple seated facing him on the French love-seat. He perceived their marriage to be a sham, a means of deceiving the straight world. Moreover, they had always detested him, opposed his relationship with Strutwick.

"I am willing to accept any living arrangement, so long as Strutwick and I are together. He declined to move into my condo with me. Told me he had always lived in this house, said he belongs here. Last year I offered to buy an island for us in the Caribbean. He refused to move there."

"Pardon me, but I don't follow the line of reasoning here." Judy interjected. "Neither Kei nor I ever advised Strut not to live with you."

"I'm aware of that! Let me finish. The other alternative is for me to move into this house, and Strutwick doesn't agree to that, either, although he isn't strongly opposed. He feels we would not be compatible, and I'm including Pamela Wilburn and Bradley Boddicker, too, when I say we."

"And our sons, John and Gerald, too. Even though they are only one and two years old," Kei said.

"They require constant attention. Their nurse also resides here...and sleeps on the same floor with the rest of us." Judy added.

"Neither Strutwick nor I are young any longer." Derrick pursued. "I have to know if we are going through the remaining years together or not. I'd like your position on my moving into Widdicombe House."

"It seems to me you're bypassing Strut's wishes," Kei said.

"Our lifestyles, yours versus the rest of us, with the exception of Strut, are very different, Mr. Agnew." Judy spoke slowly. "Kei and I would oppose your moving in."

"That's what I needed to hear. I'll modify my activities accordingly!" Derrick stood up to leave. Kei saw him to the front door.

Intending to drive to The Greene Room, Derrick changed his mind and headed north on Granby Street. When he reached the end of it, he turned right onto East Ocean View Avenue and slowed down. He was accustomed to having his way, and his desire to live with me had been thwarted. If Kei and Judy had not opposed his wish to live in Widdicombe House, their assent would have ensured my approval. Derrick knew this, and he was bitter and considered dissolving our ten and a half year relationship.

Tonight I need someone young, Derrick decided, and he began to scrutinize the men walking up the busy avenue. What was it Max always called this street? Oh, yes, the Street of Broken Dreams. After driving seven blocks, he saw a towheaded young man hitchhiking. When he stopped, the fellow hopped into the car.

"Where to?" Derrick asked, pulling back into the traffic.

"Anywheres," the lad answered. "Ah'm jist amblin' 'bout. Ain't nivver seen yuh on the street 'fore."

"You're a street hustler, right?"

"Are yuh a cop, suh?"

"Hell no! I'm a faggot! How about you, kid?"

"Ah'm lak you."

"Then let's go to my place."

"Shur. And mah name's Ezekiel Scutchings, but folks all call me Zeke."

Zeke was impressed with Derrick's condominium on the top floor of the high rise. As he walked around looking at the expensive furnishings, Derrick studied him. Zeke was handsome and sturdy with clear green eyes and naturally white-blond hair. When he grinned, there were appealing dimples in his cheeks. Finally he turned and faced the older man.

"Fifty dolluhs ain't too much, is it? Ah'll do anything fer yuh, suh."

"That's fine, but I'm warning you beforehand, Zeke. I like my sex rough!"

"Ruff? Dat's okay." Zeke answered naively. "Mista Poletti wuz mighty ruff wif me. Ah'm usta dat kinda sex."

Then he wandered onto the balcony and was captivated by the city lights below. Derrick went to stand beside the guileless young man at the railing.

"Tell me about this Poletti character. Was he your lover?"

"Naw, he's daid now. Ah wuz his sex boy fer a long time."

With Derrick's prodding, Zeke told about his life. Born in a small town in the mountains of West Virginia, he had six brothers and sisters. His father had deserted them so long ago, Zeke had no memory of him at all. His mother took in washing and cleaned for other women in order to support her family. Always tired, she didn't know that Zeke started skipping school in the second grade. Through an older boy he met Joe Poletti one day while playing hooky. The following day Poletti went to Zeke's mother and gave her money. He took Zeke back to Norfolk with him. The boy was Joe Poletti's plaything until the gambler was killed. Derrick had heard other tales about the infamous underworld character, but this was a new one.

Zeke pulled off his tee shirt. On his muscular chest were carved the initials, J and P, one over each nipple. Next, with two fingers, he pressed his upper lip away to expose his teeth. Two of the front ones were missing. Joe Poletti had become violent when he was drinking.

After Poletti died, a Mr. Finney had tried to help Zeke, but the youth went to Richmond with a fast-talking gay man, only to be dropped later. Zeke hustled and did handyman jobs in the capital city until he met Chadwick Anber, a once wealthy aristocrat who was selling his family's plantation home in Charles City County.

"Another rotting family!" Derrick sneered.

"Ah loved Mista Anber, but he died. Jist las' spring." Zeke continued. "We wuz gonna live together." He wiped away a tear.

Asking Zeke's age, Derrick was surprised that he was only twenty-one. He had been through enormous hurt, yet he could still smile, and he made money the best way he could. The young fellow's calm trust touched Derrick.

"Come on indoors, Zeke. Tonight I'll be gentle."

In the bedroom Derrick slowly removed the masculine young hustler's clothing, savoring the well-developed physique. Zeke's was no pumped-up body; hard labor had shaped it. Guiding him into his bed, Derrick made love to him tenderly.

Hours later neither of the sleeping men heard the key turn in the front door. The overhead chandelier suddenly snapped on, light glaring down on their naked bodies. They sat up abruptly, momentarily frozen there, and stared at me.

"Derrick!" I screamed, not instantly comprehending what I was seeing. "Derrick!"

"Don't lose your temper!" Derrick regained his composure. He stood up and pulled on a robe. "We'll deal with this calmly!"

"Calmly? I find you in bed with this man, and you advise me to behave calmly?" I found a chair and collapsed into it. "I'm entitled to make a scene! You have betrayed me! How long have you been bedding down with other men behind my back?"

"This was the one and only time, Strutwick! Believe me...for god's sake!" He came to stand beside my chair. "I was going to tell you about it."

"And with AIDS out there! You are reckless as well as untrue!"

"Ah ain't got it," Zeke, still on the bed, called to me.

"I saw Judy and Kei earlier tonight," Derrick said. "You and I need to talk."

"We certainly do! At least fix me a bourbon and water. And I think I'm going to need more than one!"

"Ah'll git it, suh," the towheaded young man said, hopping out of bed.

"Half and half," I directed him as his naked body left the room. "Well, he certainly isn't self-conscious!" I quipped.

"Zeke," Derrick called. "Step into your jeans."

"Why did you talk to Kei and Judy, Derrick? To tell them you were dissolving our relationship?"

"Not at all." He knelt beside my chair. "I asked them if it was acceptable with them for me to live in Widdicombe House with you...and it is not."

"I have told you that repeatedly," I said.

"But you never confronted them with it, Strutwick. Someone had to."

"And you found their reply so upsetting that you went out and snatched up a young man to take to bed?"

"You might say that, yes. It has been six and a half years since your mother died, and I have been your lover all that time." Derrick stood up and hovered over me. "Even longer. We should have been living together, but you refused. Oh, I understand your reasons, to some degree, but I have to come first."

"I love my family, Derrick."

Zeke brought me my drink and I swallowed greedily. Derrick introduced us, and the young man sat down on the side of the bed, looking at his feet and wiggling his toes. Even though I was in the midst of an emotional crisis, I was still struck by his manly beauty.

"And so you should. But, Strutwick, if I'm going to live alone, I'm going to have something on the side! I am tired of all the lonely times...when you're working and when you're with your family. I don't like having to be fitted into your schedule!"

"Derrick. you are fifty years old, and you sound like a twenty-one year old. Surely your passion isn't that overwhelming?"

"Man, I am talking about love! I adore you, Strutwick Widdicombe!" Derrick smashed a fist into his palm. "But as for the passion, that, too! I'm as hungry for it as I ever was!"

He tore off his robe, slinging it aside,. and inhaled deeply. His rock-hard chest was well-defined and his small stomach corded. His arms and legs were masses of thick muscle. Derrick's years of handball had kept his powerful body fit.

"Fifty years old or not," he shouted, glancing at the young man sitting on the bed, "I've still got a prime body, and this twenty-one year old found it exciting enough!"

"Ah nivver had sex wif anybody batter," Zeke said softly.

I stood up and walked to the bedroom door. Derrick, still naked, followed me, taking my arm.

"I love you, Strutwick, and all I'm asking this morning is that you don't make any rash decisions."

"I do not intend to. I'm tired and wish to go to bed."

Claire's death six and a half years ago had stunned Kei, Mrs. O'Brian, and me. Kei relied heavily on Judy, Bradley, and Pam for support. Poor Mrs. O'Brian fell apart and took to her bed until the funeral. As for myself, I leaned on Derrick who saw me through the dark days. He had sufficient inner strength for both of us. Jessie Cobb's death was an added painful loss.

After the funerals, both Kei and I were gently led back into our routines.

Kei and Bradley were already graduates of Washington and Lee and of the University of Richmond respectively. Kei was administrative manager of Trilling Industrial Park, and Judy guided him back into his responsibilities there. Between Judy and Bradley, now the executive manager of Trilling Mall, Kei was sustained until the deadening grief subsided.

Derrick drove me to The Greene Room and stayed near me. Loyal Max and my manager, Sam Zole, further supported me.

For years to come I would not allow marzipan, fruitcake, egg nog, or rum balls in the house at Christmas time. Claire's favorite Yuletide treats, as she had referred to them, were painful memories.

Heartsick and handicapped by arthritis, Mrs. O'Brian resumed her duties, but she confided to me that she wished to retire. She was seventy-one and had devoted her life to our family. Now she wanted to spend her remaining years with her sister in Bowling Green, Virginia.

I called a family conference that night. After we settled ourselves in the drawing room, I presented Mrs. O'Brian's request to the others.

"At her age she deserves to retire with dignity," Judy said.

"It's mighty hard to think of my world without her in it." Kei spoke up. "She has been a strength in my life...even before I moved into Widdicombe House."

"She has been an important part of my entire life," I said, "administering to my childhood bumps and bruises, drying my tears with a corner of her apron. I will be dismayed when she leaves."

"Mrs. O'Brian was always there for you," Bradley was sympathetic, "even more so than Claire was."

"But like it or not," Pam said, "the one inevitable thing in life is change."

"Again, we'll have to brace ourselves, Strut," Kei concluded. "There is only one right course."

"I realize."

"She should receive a pension," Judy said. "I'll pay half."

"And I the other half." I added.

We discussed the amount. The bar was doing well, and I could afford to be generous. The next household business was in regard to whom we could employ to take over Mrs. O'Brian's duties. No one could replace her; it was the business of cooking and of overseeing the housekeeping that we addressed.

"There may be Dougan." I suggested. "He cooked for me at The Greene Room when he first moved here from Carolina. Has his own little café now on Monticello Avenue."

"Sounds as though he has his hands full already," Bradley said.

"His little place has never caught on," I answered. "Delicious home-cooked meals, reasonable prices. Derrick and I have eaten there a number of times."

"Norfolk is saturated with good restaurants." Pam commented.

"Why don't you speak to him, Strut?" Judy asked. "If you say he's a good cook, that's sufficient recommendation for me."

Before going to The Greene Room, I stopped off at Dougan's café. The twenty-seven year old man accepted my offer, grateful to close his place. It had been a losing proposition. Moreover, his lover, Ross, who was two years older, wanted the job as housekeeper. On the first of the month they moved into two rooms on the third floor of Widdicombe House. They furnished a living room and a bedroom with their own possessions.

Mrs. O'Brian thoroughly trained both young men. She took a fancy to Dougan and even gave him her special recipes. Ross proved to be adept at overseeing the two maids. They respected him and worked diligently to please him. The time came when Mrs. O'Brian knew she had completed her instruction, and goodbyes were distressing for us. On a rainy April morning Pam drove her to

Bowling Green.

According to Claire's written instructions, Judy became custodian of the family jewels, with directions to present various pieces to future Widdicombe brides. Until that time she was to avail herself freely of all the antique jewelry.

The week after Mrs. O'Brian left, the second floor sleeping arrangements changed. Judy and Pam moved into Claire's two-room suite, and Bradley shifted his clothes and personal effects across the hall into Kei's bedroom. The other three rooms were now vacant. It was the first floor that, with the exception of my bedroom, retained a heterosexual facade. Derrick did sometimes slip into my bed in the wee hours via the walled garden.

The Greene Room turned a nice profit in the following years, and I repaid the money Derrick had loaned me.

In family conference one Sunday after dinner, Judy offered to change the names of her industrial park and her shopping mall from Trilling to Widdicombe. Kei and I both hesitated. For moments there was an uncomfortable silence.

"It was your business acumen that built them, Judy," I said. "As far as I'm concerned, they are rightfully named. After all, The Greene Room did not become 'Strut's Place'."

"Hardly the same," Judy laughed. "My point is that there are no longer Trillings in Norfolk. Mother's remarried, living on the west coast, and I'm a Widdicombe now."

"To change the names to Widdicombe would be a break with tradition, Judy." Kei began to explain. "Our family has always been peculiar about its name. It has never been on public signs or up in lights...or rather in neon. The Widdicombes shy away from ostentatious display."

"I think I understand," Judy said quietly. "I really do. It wouldn't be fitting for the family to splash its name across commercial enterprises. How silly of me not to have realized it. We won't change a thing."

But some things did change. Kei and Judy began a pattern of entertaining influential professional and business people. Dinners were scheduled on a regular basis. Judy was making money, hand over fist, in land speculation and development. These social contacts were an integral part of her commercial success.

Pam, Bradley, and I did not attend these functions, although we could have. Kei and Judy felt the need to play straight couple in order for her to make more money, and they were most likely Norfolk's most prominent couple. Pam, Bradley, and I did not feel obligated to participate.

In time Kei and Judy augmented their straight couple act. Artificial insemination was obtained in D.C., and they became a family. Gerald was born in 1986 and John in 1987. The Widdicombe name would be perpetuated. Even though I felt certain fulfillment in this, the babies further distanced me from their parents. I wondered if my gay lifestyle was too open.

Pam had secured a Mrs. Acree to be the boys' nurse. In her youth Pam had known Mrs. Acree's daughter, a lesbian. The older woman had been accepting of her daughter's sexuality and had welcomed her friends in their home. Now the second floor bedrooms were all occupied again, Mrs. Acree's room was between the separate bedrooms of Gerald and John.

A few months after John's birth I was sitting alone in the gazebo, enjoying the summer foliage there in the walled garden. My life was good now, but there was still the perpetual problem with Derrick.

He never ceased insisting that we live together. I could not move him into Widdicombe House; he would clash with Kei and Judy. It would become a house divided against itself, and I would surely be trapped at the center of the tumult. Derrick was right in claiming we should live together, yet I could not leave my home. It was a part of me and I of it.

"You're miles away, Strut. Care for company?"

I jumped at the sound of Pam's voice. Lost in thought I had not noticed her come through the family dining room's French doors. As she approached me, her easy stride lifted my spirits.

"Please do," I called. "It's pleasant in the garden this afternoon."

"I don't see enough of you." She pecked me on the cheek and sat beside me. "You are always at The Greene Room or at Derrick's, it seems."

"Where are Kei and Judy?" I smiled. "The house seems almost empty."

"At the Botetourt Yacht and Country Club again. They were

invited to a wedding and reception."

"And Bradley? He, too?"

"Oh, no!" Pam grinned. "Bradley went over to his grandfather's. He's worn out with all that socializing."

"Then there are three of us. I sometimes feel it separates us."

"I'm sure you do. Judy and Kei spend so much time with straight people." Pam hunched over, clasping her hands together between her knees. "After working five days a week, there isn't a lot of time left to spend with Judy. All this mixing with straights leaves even less."

"How insensitive of me to complain! Of course it is much more difficult for you than it is for me."

"It's the reason for the only serious quarrel we've ever had, Strut. But what can I do? I'm in love with the woman."

"And she's in love with you. Be patient for now."

"You're lucky that Derrick rejects that sort of a life."

"He treats me like a prince."

"In a way you are. Some people worship the ground you Widdicombes walk on."

"Derrick and I are mavericks, both of us. We are not acceptable to polite society, Pam."

"I think I admire that trait most of all." Pam ran her fingers through her short blonde hair.

"I take after one or two of the former Widdicombes. What's bred in the bone is born in the flesh. We are a curious breed."

"Want to go out for dinner with me?" She changed the subject. "I don't feel like being alone right now."

"I'd be delighted, ma'am. Give me twenty minutes to freshen up."

In the powder room I scrutinized my face. It was slightly puffy, and there were tiny crow's feet at the corners of my eyes. The youthful look was gone. The bloom was off the rose, as Claire might have said. I was moving along through the years, I had thought at the time, yet I had been relieved that Derrick still found me appealing.

Driving back from Derrick's condominium, I tried to convince myself that it was natural for Derrick to want a little on the side.

Most men are like that, I decided. Derrick and I had a marriage-type of arrangement, and marriage is an unnatural state. Why, this Zeke is as butch as Derrick is. It cannot possibly last. Moreover, I vowed to remove the cotton-haired hillbilly from our lives. After all, he is a hustler. There is more than one way to skin a cat.

CHAPTER TEN

"Pick up the phone, Mr. Widdicombe!" Dougan was hammering on the door and shouting. "He says it's important."

"All right!" I called out as I sat up in my bed.

My head throbbed. Glancing at the china clock, now keeping excellent time, I shuddered. It was eight twenty-one. I picked up my bedside extension reluctantly.

"1 have slept only four hours! Who is this?"

"Sam Zole, Strut. I wouldn't wake you this early, but it's urgent."

I strained to become alert; Sam had never called me at home before afternoon; he knew my hours.

"It's Max." he continued. "He's in the hospital...bad off. It's pneumonia. I brought him in at three this morning."

"Which hospital?" I was now wide awake. "Are you there now?"

I dressed and rushed over to Tidewater General. Sam was sitting beside Max's bed.

"He hasn't worked in the bar for several nights," I said. "I thought it was just a severe cold."

"Me, too, Strut."

I could tell Sam was worried. Max looked terrible. His eyes were closed, and his face was splotchy. A breathing apparatus covered his nose and mouth. It was connected to an oxygen tank. He was sucking hard for the air.

"Can Max hear us?" I asked, moving close to the bed and taking his hand.

"I think so."

I knelt next to the bed. "Aren't you the sleepy one?" I said lightly. "How long is my business partner going to lie in this bed?"

We watched Max's face; it remained expressionless. Then, ever so slightly, he pressed my hand.

"I intend to stand by you until you are well, Max." 1 almost whispered. "Fight the good fight for me...for Sam and me."

A doctor opened the door and motioned for us to step into the hall. When we did he informed us that they were testing Max's blood for AIDS. I was horrified. The physician asked a few questions and informed us that Max might not survive. I agreed to see that the medical expenses were paid in the event Max had no health insurance. The doctor seemed distant. Then he was gone.

"Sam, you can manage without me at The Greene Room, can't your?"

"No problem. I'll make the bank deposits, too."

"Then I will stay with Max until he is better or..." I did not complete the sentence.

"But get your rest, Strut. To be strong for Max, you'll need it."

After Sam left, I went back into the room. I dampened a wash cloth and wiped Max's face as best I could. Then I called home and explained the situation to Dougan. He was concerned and wanted to help, but there was nothing he could do for Max right now. Dougan assured me that he would advise the family of my whereabouts.

Next I phoned Derrick and told him. He wanted to come to Tidewater General immediately, saying that Zeke had left his condo earlier. I asked Derrick to wait until that night.

I hung up and leaned over Max. He was still gasping for air, his eyes still closed. The poor fellow hadn't had much of a life. Bingo Jarman had been combination father-mother-lover to him. After Bingo had died, all Max had was The Greene Room and anonymous sex with hustlers.

He had never wanted another lover after Bingo. I did not understand that. Although Max was forty-one now, he looked ten years younger. It would have been easy for him to have another relationship.

Time passed slowly in the little room, with only the sound of Max sucking in oxygen. I held his hand and continued to speak to him, just to let him know I was there and that I cared.

At seven o'clock there was a knock on the door. Pam and Bradley had come. She beckoned for me to step outside.

"Will he make it?" Pam asked, kissing me on the cheek.

"Don't know yet," I said, a lump forming In my throat.

"Derrick and I talked. In a few minutes he'll be here to take you out to eat. You must be starved."

"I forgot about eating," I said, suddenly hungry.

"Tell me what to do and then go down to the lobby. Derrick will meet you there."

"Are you sure you want to stay?"

"I'm sure and don't argue with me about it, Strut."

"Wipe his forehead, and, if you can, talk to him, encourage him."

"I can."

Pam reached for the door handle, but Bradley stopped her. I looked at him. He was terrified.

"I can't go in there!" He was shaking. "He may have AIDS! I'm afraid!"

"You won't catch it if it's AIDS, Bradley." Pam assured him. "Has to be an exchange of body fluids...or through a tainted blood transfusion." We both explained the lack of danger. Finally he summoned sufficient courage, and they went into Max's room.

When Derrick met me in the hospital lobby, he threw his arms around me and hugged me, not giving a happy damn what others thought. I was grateful; I needed that hug.

In the car Derrick asked questions. I told him the little I knew.

"Stop worrying for now, Strutwick. It can't help," He reached his right hand over and squeezed my shoulder. "And dinner? Would you like seafood?'

"Yes, I would like seafood very much," I answered, "but tell me about Zeke. Are you going to see him again?"

"For the time being we will not discuss Zeke...at all," he said firmly. "'We have all we can deal with in helping Max."

I accepted that and mentally placed the problem of Zeke on hold. Dinner refreshed me, and I felt close to Derrick once again.

Back at the hospital, Pam, Derrick, Bradley, and I had a conference outside Max's room. Bradley had done beautifully, Pam informed us, his gentle demeanor shining through.

All three of them insisted on helping with Max, and a schedule was worked out. Derrick would spend nights, staying from eleven until seven. Bradley would relieve him and stay until ten. He was going to go into work late but was sure that would be no problem. At ten I would arrive, to be relieved at six by Pam who insisted on staying until eleven. Max would always have one of us with him.

"I truly think he hears me when I talk to him." Bradley spoke up. "I feel it."

"He does." I answered, "I'm sure."

"Hearing is the last sense a sick person loses," Pam said. "I've read that somewhere."

Before going home I went in to have a few minutes more with Max. I stroked his arm and told him that Derrick would be with him through the night.

Dougan sent me back to the hospital the next day carrying a hamper of food. Making sure I was well-fed was a trait he had in common with Mrs. O'Brian. When I relieved Bradley, Max was still in the same condition.

That afternoon the doctor informed me that Max had pneumocystis pneumonia and indeed did have AIDS. Again I felt that this physician was cool and indifferent.

"Might not make it," he said as he terminated our conversation. "Best to let his family know."

"He hasn't any." I replied to the man's back as he walked away.

When Derrick came by to take me to dinner, I related my experiences with the doctor. Derrick was irritated. The next day Max had another doctor. Derrick had made phone calls.

Pam had left her prayer book at the hospital, and I read and prayed a lot of the time. On the fourth day Max opened his eyes and his breathing improved. Then the nurses began removing his oxygen mask for short periods of time, even though it was kept close at hand. I did not allow Max to talk very much. It tired him.

The road back was slow, butt the time finally came when Max could go home. The doctor was adamant, however, in insisting that someone be with him. Derrick made a suggestion that caught me off guard.

"Zeke can move in with Max, and be there to cook and look after him. That's a big room up there over the bar."

"Why, there is only one bed, Derrick." I protested. "It is preferable for Max to go to Widdicombe House. Mrs. O'Brian's room is available."

We were sitting in Derrick's car, parked in front of The Greene Room. With Max so improved I had decided to go to the bar and give Sam Zole the night off. He had more than earned it.

"Max won't be happy at Widdicombe House; he wasn't when you took him there after Bingo Jarman died. Don't you remember?"

"But why do you want Zeke involved in this?"

"I want Zeke off the streets, and this is a job he can handle. Furthermore, I'll buy a single bed and send it over."

"Oh, all right! Have it sent over then. If it means getting a hustler out of that line of work, I won't object."

Derrick put his hand on my leg. The warmth of it thrilled me, and I longed to make love with him. Max's pneumonia had left no time for Derrick and me to share intimate moments.

"You'll find Zeke is a capable handyman, Strutwick."

"How much is he going to cost me?"

"I'll pay his wages. That way I will be helping Max and Zeke, too."

I got out of Derrick's car and started toward The Greene Room, but he called to me. Walking back to the automobile, I paused by his window.

"Strutwick, remember that I love you very much."

"And I love you...but I have a question."

"Sure."

"Are you and Zeke still making out?"

Derrick looked at me strangely. It was the only time I ever saw him look self-conscious. I waited for an answer, but he remained silent. Then I turned and went inside the bar.

Two days later Max was discharged from the hospital. It was a beautiful day, and he was excited as I drove him home...home to The Greene Room. "I like the big buildings, Strut."

"Norfolk hasn't much of a skyline."

"Skyscrapers?" He leaned his head outside the car window. "I see some."

"A few. Richmond has more. What Norfolk has is not so much buildings as it has a special feeling. Once someone has lived here for a while, he starts to pick up on it."

"You're right, Strut. I wouldn't live anywhere else."

"Look at that azure sky. It's a Norfolk sky, Max. And those feathery clouds. Why, Kei and Judy's wedding cake wasn't iced so beautifully."

I stopped the car in front of the bar and Sam came out to meet us. We very slowly helped Max inside and up the stairs. He was very weak.

"I want Zeke to take you for a walk each day, Max. You need to rebuild your strength."

"Think Zeke can cook grits?" Max asked. "I sure did miss grits with my eggs and bacon in the hospital."

"If he can't, then I'll teach him," Sam said. "Remember, Max, he's here to look after you."

"Ask Sam about your Street of Broken Dreams, Max." I smiled. "He travels it most nights after the bar closes."

"Trying to take my place, Sam?" Max was amused. "I can't let you do that!"

"Oh, no, I'm not cruising." Sam answered. "I'm seeing a guy regularly...great guy, too. He lives out in Ocean View. Owns his own beach cottage. I'm moving up in the world!"

"Honk your horn at the boys for me when you ride past them, Sam. I miss 'em, but I won't be back. Can't take a chance on infecting anybody." Kindhearted Max never considered the truth. A hustler had infected him.

CHAPTER ELEVEN

I closed the family journals and stood up. Max would he leaving to keep his doctor's appointment, and I wanted to be at The Greene Room when he did. Passing out of the library and choosing a lightweight jacket, I could hear Judy and Pam arguing somewhere upstairs. I went to my car in the carriage house. It was a beautiful October day, and the brisk autumn air was invigorating. It braced me for the execution of my plan. Today I intended to rid myself of my rival.

Sam Zole's car was still in the parking lot when I reached the bar. I hurried inside and went upstairs. Sam and Zeke were with Max who was putting on his coat. They hadn't expected me.

"Going with us, Strut? Be glad to have the company," Sam said.

"Not this time. I intend to have Zeke repair a few things while you are gone."

"Shur, Mista Strut. Ah'm right handy."

After Sam and Max drove off, Zeke and I remained upstairs.

"I recommend old clothes, Zeke. Best not soil your new apparel."

Zeke nodded and began undressing. I knew his sport clothes had been purchased by Derrick who was beginning to dote on the lad. Shirtless, he presented a muscular torso that could excite almost any gay man. Yet he was marred. There were someone's initials carved on his chest, and I suppressed an impulse to inquire about them. He unbuckled his belt and unzipped his trousers. As soon as he had stepped out of them, I moved toward him. His green eyes widened.

"You are a very attractive man." I complimented him. "Anyone would be honored to go to bed with you."

I put a hand lightly on his broad shoulder, then let it slide slowly down his arm and rest on his hard bicep. He looked frightened.

"Please doan, Mista Strut. Ah gotta skedaddle on downstairs tuh do sum work fer yuh."

"Easy, Zeke, don't fret. This is acceptable. After all, I *am* Derrick's lover."

I encircled his small waist with my arms and pressed his body into mine. He hardened instinctively.

"Shur, but ah promised Derrick ah'd be faithful tuh him."

I brushed my lips over his, but he turned his head away.

"Then we will not divulge our secret." I ran my fingers over his buttocks. They firmed under my touch. "You were a hustler, Zeke. Did a John ever offer you two hundred dollars before? That's what I'll pay you for sex."

"Naw, nivver!" His voice was husky. "But ah cain't!" He wrenched free of my embrace. "Mah body belongs tuh Derrick. Ah's his'n."

My attempt to seduce Zeke did not work, but I was not ready to admit defeat. Determined to remove him from Derrick's life, I played my trump card.

"Then I'll be honest with you," I said coldly. "Derrick and I have been lovers for a long time, and you are a threat, a very serious threat, to our relationship."

"Huh, me?" He stood there and looked bewildered, wearing only his little white socks.

"I am prepared to give you ten thousand dollars to leave Tidewater. To depart from Derrick's life forever. We can go to my bank right now, and I will put the money in your hands."

Zeke gasped in disbelief. "I nivver seed that kind uh money 'fore!"

"You can get yourself a college education...become a learned man!"

He paced the floor, pressing his hands together. I secretly marveled at the rippling of his powerful calves as he walked. This twenty-one year old was so unaware of his own intensely desirable body.

"Ah ain't had much book-larning, Mista Strut. Mah brain doan work so good." He stopped pacing and faced me. "Ah hafta git hep from uh bright teacher!"

"New clothes, a car...think of what ten thousand dollars can do!"

"Thar's nuthin ah wants tuh do 'cep stay wif Derrick." Zeke ran his fingers through his white hair, "He laks me uh heap."

I struggled to control the rage that surged inside me. I had thought everyone had his price, but this simple man was beyond temptation. "Then your answer is no, firmly no?"

"'Tis no, fer shur," he nodded to me as he planted his large feet wide apart in an unyielding stance,

"Don't tell Derrick or anybody else about all this. Now get something on, and I'll put you to work. Can you fix a leaky spigot?"

Even though Max was vastly improved, his doctor wanted someone always within earshot. A loud buzzer was installed behind The Greene Room's main bar, connecting to a button by Max's bed upstairs. This freed Zeke, to a great extent. Although he continued to be with Max during the hours the bar was closed, he began spending evenings at Derrick's condominium.

New Years fell on a weekend that year, and I persuaded Derrick to celebrate it with me out of town. Leaving Zeke behind for a few days was a comfort to me. We checked into the newly refurbished Jefferson Hotel in Richmond. After dinner we partied at a private club and welcomed the commencement of 1989 in each other's arms.

In the late morning of New Year's Day we ravenously ate big breakfasts provided by room service. For the first time in half a year I was happy. Derrick was sitting upright in the large hotel bed. I positioned my head in his lap and gazed up at him.

"We should take little holidays together more often, Derrick," I said. "This has been perfect. I feel our love has been renewed."

"It could be this way forever, Strutwick," he answered, "if you would live with me. I think you know that."

"And your hillbilly? Would he still be your boy-toy?"

"Zeke? My answer today is no, but I can't speak for tomorrow."

"What do you mean? I am yours for the rest of my life, unless you cast me aside. Why can't you make the same commitment to me?"

"I would if I truly had you, but I don't." Derrick stroked my cheeks. "I'm compelled to share you with your family and all the ghosts of your aristocratic ancestors. And with the majesty of Widdicombe House. That is where your true commitment rests."

"That isn't fair, Derrick. You knew my life was composed of all that when you first sought a relationship with me."

"That I did, but I believed you would give our love top priority.

Instead, I'm fitted into your life, not the central part of it."

I sat up and reached for my robe. Again we had reached the same impasse.

"Therefore I cannot say what importance Zeke will have in my life in the future." After a moment he continued. "I do grow fonder of him daily."

"I don't know how you relate to him." I rose and poured a cup of luke-warm coffee from the silver coffeepot. "It is as though he speaks another language."

"There is no need for you to relate to Zeke. He is blindly devoted to me." Derrick stood up and began dressing. "That, from a handsome and muscular young man, is sufficient."

I sat in a chair by the window, sipping my coffee and watching the traffic outside.

"He is intellectually inferior to you, Derrick. Can you be content with such a man?"

"Intellectual companionship can be found elsewhere. Zeke is my delight."

'Then our romance is in serious difficulty." I turned my head to look into his eyes. "I don't know how to let go of you."

"Then work it out, Strutwick. Only you can do that."

"You want be to break with family, my heritage?"

"Not break with...distance yourself from. If you don't, you may find out that old glory is a poor companion in your bed on cold winter nights."

"Oh, Derrick!" I turned and looked again at the cars passing below on Sin Street. "I don't want to discuss this any longer."

I felt insecure and vaguely afraid. The thought of growing old without Derrick was unpleasant. He had emotionally supported me ever since Claire's death. He came to stand behind my chair, resting his hands on my shoulders.

"We won't speak of this any longer. It was not my intention to issue an ultimatum." His voice softened, "Tell me about Max. Is he still growing stronger?'

"He is doing splendidly. A perfect patient, too...obeys the doctor's every utterance. To be prepared, however, he has made his will. His share of The Greene Room is to go to Sam Zole when he dies."

"That's fifty per cent, isn't it, Strutwick? How do you feel about co-ownership with Sam, should it come to that?"

"Perfectly fine. Sam is a gem, and I would welcome such a partnership. I feel, though, that Max may survive AIDS. There are new drugs coming forth."

"God, I hope he does. He's a sweet little guy. But be prepared for the worst while you hope for the best."

"I will. Meanwhile he must enjoy life. He has asked me to take him to the Azalea Festival in April. He's never been,"

"Do it, Strutwick. You won't regret it."

It was after eleven o'clock when I walked into Widdicombe House. The first floor was empty. Depositing my luggage in my bedroom, I wandered in to the music room and turned on the lights. The mellow wood of the grand piano glowed. I impulsively ran my fingers over it, imagining my grandmother seated there on the piano bench in an elegant evening gown and glittering family jewels. Her small fingers moved over the keyboard as she played Berlioz's "Symphonic Fantastique." Hushed ladies and gentlemen in straight-backed French chairs listened intently. Then the envisioned scene faded, and I was standing there alone. This had been my grandmother's piano; the family journals described her fine musical ability.

Leaving the music room, I walked into the still lighted drawing room. Freshly cut flowers in china vases were in abundance. I remembered Judy and Kei having said they would be entertaining guests on New Year's Day. Now everyone had gone, and the beautiful room was empty.

I recalled the night before Oliver's funeral more than eighteen years ago. Dear Jessie Cobb had rattled on about her family, their success and misfortunes. Neil, not yet my lover, conversed with eleven-year old Kei about basketball. Claire and I were savoring our newly forged bond, and talked to our guests about everything except the reason they had come: Oliver's suicide. The memory of that night was etched in my brain.

How much our lives had changed since that night. The urgent need for money had been satisfied, and Kei had married Judy Trilling, insuring the family of a large fortune. Claire and Jessie had died in a plane crash, and I had abused Neil's love.

Now there were other problems. Judy and Kei were neglecting their lovers to further deepen their entrenchment into Norfolk's business world. They were constantly scrambling for more dollars. It was regrettable that they could not relax and enjoy what they already had. As for my dilemma, I would lose Derrick if I didn't live with him, leave Widdicombe House to share my life with him.

Should I abandon so much of what contributed to my being the person I am? Was there any guarantee that Derrick would eject Zeke from our lives if I did? Would there be other young men, needed by Derrick to please his vanity and satisfy his lust? My observations were that relationships did not last. Claire's and Carolyn's didn't. Neither did Vic's, nor Neil's. Yet the Widdicombe family did endure, still endures. It had moved through the centuries in Norfolk. For me, nothing superceded my position in it.

I decided I must be getting old. How long had I stood there, reliving the past, pondering my future? The dread of losing Derrick was paralyzing, but I resolved to get on with my life.

I walked into the vestibule and saw Kei coming down the stairs. He was grim-faced.

"Kei, where is everyone?"

"We're upstairs in Judy's parlor. I've been sent to see if you were home. Pam and Judy want you to join us...in a discussion we're having."

"A family conference on New Year's night? My, it must be serious."

"It is. Come up with me, please."

We ascended the staircase together. At twenty-nine, Kei was a handsome man, but the solemn expression on his young face disturbed me. Entering the sitting room, I looked at Judy and Pam. Their expressions were even more dismal than Kei's. When Judy greeted me, her smile was quick and forced. Pam's was painfully weak.

"Please sit down, Strut. Your input is needed," Judy informed me. "Pam and I are examining our priorities, our relationship."

"And you want me to hear this?" I sat down. "Isn't it a personal situation?'

"Yes, very," Judy continued, "but we can't resolve it alone. We've tried, and we get nowhere."

"I want your input." Pam spoke up. "We both do."

"In one sense it is a family matter." Kei sat down beside Judy on a love-seat. They were facing Pam and me, seated in chairs. "The family is, as Pam feels, at the center of the problem."

"Then I imagine I am part of the problem." I answered. "Please divulge the privileged information."

"No, you're not part of the problem!" Pam reached over and pressed my arm. "We know you'll understand."

"Strut," Judy began, "Pam wants me to spend more time with her and less with people in the business and professional circles. We have argued about this before...several times. She doesn't understand that such connections mean money in the bank for all of us."

"I do understand, Judy." Pam protested. "There's just no time left over for the two of us."

"And today we had guests in, Strut," Kei added, "to celebrate New Years. Pam thinks Judy should have spent the day with her."

"She should have. New Years is special...a new beginning, sort of. It's a time for relationships to start anew, too." Pam countered. She ran her hands through her short hair and then clasped them together between her knees. I knew she was frustrated.

"This is the second time today I have been a party to relationship examination. Derrick and I did ours in Richmond."

"Did you resolve anything?" Pam asked hopefully.

"No, we did not. He told me I allow my aristocratic heritage to be a millstone around my neck, but let's continue with the matter at hand. Judy, you are already quite wealthy. I don't know your exact net worth and don't wish to. My question is, how much is enough? Can you set a goal in dollars and then ease up on work and entertaining, once you reach it?"

Judy stood up and moved to the marble mantle. She rested one delicate hand by an old Wedgewood vase.

"No one can answer that question, Strut. There are variables involved. There's future inflation as well as educational expenses for Gerald and John."

"I understand," I said, "but there are CDs and municipal bonds and Lord knows what else. I do not pretend to be the business person you are, but I think you could create a financial safety net.

Pam needs to know when she can have her own quality time with you."

"We do have our special moments together, Strut!"

"Not many." Pam corrected her, "Judy, I love you! When you come to bed nights, you're so exhausted, you fall asleep immediately!" Silent tears rolled down Pam's cheeks.

"What I'm doing is for you, too, Pam. Why don't you understand that?"

"Because I want *you*, not money! You are worth more to me than all the money in Virginia!"

"And, Strut," Judy focused on me again, "have you forgotten what kind of financial condition you were in when I married Kei? You probably would have gone under!"

"No, I don't think so." I stood up and put my hands behind my back. "I am grateful for all you have done...and are doing, Judy, but if you hadn't married Kei, I most likely would have moved Derrick into the house. He would have taken over the household expenses."

"And funded my education, too?" Kei's temper flared. "I think not!"

"No, but he would have loaned me the money. Derrick is generous, Kei."

"Now hear me out, all of you!" Judy ordered. "Ever since I was a very little girl, I heard about the renowned Widdicombe family, its splendor, its aristocratic past. I grew up fiercely admiring the Widdicombes and this grand old house. Your heritage surpassed that of merely mottled families. I was deeply honored to marry into it; I still am. And I'm going to see that the Widdicombes never have economic problems again!"

"No matter how long it takes?" I asked her.

"No matter how long!" Judy raised her voice. "And that does not mean I don't love Pamela!"

"But where is love?" Pam said. "I have your companionship so seldom."

"We won't resolve this tonight." Kei stood up.

"Maybe never." Pam almost whispered.

We were tired and knew we were not resolving the problem, so we dispersed and I started down the stairs. Halfway down Pam called to me to wait. We descended together and then stood looking at each other there in the vestibule. She looked defeated.

"It's not going to change, Strut. Everything is going to go on just the same."

"I don't dare say it may not. In fact, I don't know what to say, Pam, except that I love you and wish you were happy."

"Bradley avoided the family conference. I had asked him to be there."

"He feels the same as you do?"

"Oh, yes, but he'll accept anything to be near Kei. Anything! He is miserable, though. Complains constantly to me."

"I don't think he'll ever stand up to Kei."

She broke down and wept. Taking her in my arms, I tried to comfort her.

CHAPTER TWELVE

During the next few months, Max gained strength, Pam and Judy's relationship continued to deteriorate, and I made my last will and testament. The deed of trust to Widdicombe House was held jointly by Kei and myself; therefore, I bequeathed my half to him. My half of The Greene Room I willed to Sam Zole, and my money, however much or little there might ultimately be, I left to Gerald and John, my grandnephews. I felt strange excluding Derrick from my will, but I was acceding to his directions. He had said he wanted me, not my worldly possessions.

By April, Max was excited about attending the thirty-sixth annual International Azalea Festival. I had discussed this with Max's doctor who encouraged Max's attending the events. The physician's feelings were that Max should enjoy his life, not worry about the possibility of picking up harmful germs, which might happen anywhere.

The festival honors the North Atlantic Treaty organization, usually referred to as NATO, whose Supreme Allied Command is based in Norfolk. The honored country this year was Turkey, which presented NATO with a lovely young queen.

At eleven o'clock on Friday morning, she and her court, as well as the mayor and other dignitaries, arrived in a swarm of white limousines. Max and I watched her regal entrance on the arm of a Marine escort.

Sitting in our folding chairs, we had an excellent view of the proceedings. One of our local state senators, seated behind us, made it a point to get my attention and to ask about Kei and Judy. A Navy band played the national anthem of each NATO member before its flag was raised. Max and I whispered to each other about an especially handsome young clarinet player.

Later we walked through the Norfolk Botanical Gardens. It was in full bloom, and Max was delighted with its beauty. "This is something I'll always remember, Strut. I never had such fun in my life!"

"We should have done this years ago," I said. "Didn't know you were interested."

"Oh, I was so wrapped up in the bar, I didn't think about stuff like this. Guess I became sorta one-track after Bingo died."

"Then enjoy the now, Max."

We toured a Turkish frigate moored at Waterside and visited a Turkish bazaar. Max became short-winded easily, and I insisted periodically that we stop and rest. Max would have pushed on until he dropped if I hadn't.

By ten o'clock the next morning we were downtown on Plume Street for the parade. It started to rain. I was apprehensive about Max, but we were invited to the second floor of an office building by Mister Gilmore, Vic's father. From there we had an excellent view of the parade.

The air show by the Blue Angels was postponed because of the inclement weather. These jets were the Navy's precision flying team. Flying F/A18 Hornets, they could provide a spectacular show.

The coronation of queen Azalea XXXVI was moved from the gardens to Norfolk's oldest high school. I was grateful to get Max indoors. The stage and corridors were lined with tubs of red, white, and pink azaleas. Max was as enthusiastic as a child when the queen was crowned. I particularly enjoyed the military escorts of the court.

Max wasn't interested in the City of Norfolk Ball that night, so we stopped for a seafood dinner before going back to the bar. Zeke was waiting for us.

"The only thing I missed was the Blue Angels, Zeke," Max said. "Maybe I can see them next year."

"Ah heered hit wuz put off tuh tumorra, but yuh'll see 'em. Derrick saiz he wants tuh take yuh tuh the base tuh see hit."

"That's great! You'll go, too, won't you?"

Zeke nodded, and then I said good night and started home. The Azalea Festival had been fun. Max had delighted in it; I hadn't attended for years. Now I was tired and intended to go to bed early.

My plans changed, however, when I walked into the house. Kei and Bradley were sitting in the family dining room waiting for me. They stood up when I came in.

"Strut, there's something you need to know," Bradley said. "We've had such turmoil here today!"

"It's been hell," Kei added. "Pam moved out. She and Judy are through."

"The moment I have dreaded." I held up my hand to quiet them. "Allow me fortification first. I'm fatigued." It seemed I found refuge now in following routine when all else was disturbed.

I prepared a strong bourbon and water and then led them into the library. Closing the sliding doors, we settled into deep leather chairs. I sipped my libation.

"Now, please tell me what happened."

"Pam left work very early today and came home...to pack and move out. She evidently meant to avoid a confrontation with Judy, but it didn't work out that way." Kei related the circumstances. "Judy arrived before Pam had packed all her things in her car. There was a shouting match, and Judy went into hysterics. I was summoned home by Ross. By then Pam was gone, and Judy was lying on her bed, weeping."

"Pam resigned her job with Trilling, and Judy was screaming that Pam would never get a job in Virginia again, that she'd see to it," Bradley chimed in.

"Do either of you know where Pam is now?" I asked.

"She wouldn't tell Judy where she was going," Kei answered, "but I think you'll know. She gave Ross this envelope to pass on to you. He gave it to me."

Kei took a sealed envelope from his shirt pocket and handed it to me.

I put it in my coat pocket without so much as a glance at it.

"Don't tell us what's in it, Strut," Kei nodded. "We don't want to know."

"I agree. It would be futile for you to contact her, and you shouldn't withhold her whereabouts from Judy if you do know."

"Judy doesn't know about the envelope. Don't tell her," Bradley said. "Ross won't."

"How is Judy now? Does she have a grip on her emotions?"

"After she stopped crying, she just lay there on her bed staring at the wall." Kei explained. "She looked so exhausted we decided to call a doctor."

"Mrs. Acree suggested Dr. Kibbey, a woman," Bradley said. "She's new to Tidewater. Mrs. Acre. goes to her."

"And I thought doctors didn't make house calls any longer!" I exclaimed.

"For us, some do," said Bradley.

In less than a half hour Dr. Allene Kibbey arrived and was shown upstairs by Kei. The three of us then waited in the library until she came down. Kei ushered her into the library.

"Mrs. Widdicombe is resting now. I gave her a sedative and want her to drink plenty of liquids the next few days. She's slightly dehydrated."

The tall woman spoke sternly. I found her authoritative and cold. When she spoke to us, she seemed distant and totally lacking, I thought, in a bedside manner.

"No work until after I see her in my office on Tuesday. I'll give you a prescription for Valium."

"Perhaps *you* should tell her not to work, Dr. Kibbey," Kei said. "She's pretty headstrong and—"

"I already have, Mr. Widdicombe! She promised me she will stay home and relax."

After Allene Kibbey left, we looked at each other, all three of us thinking the same thing. How had she overcome Judy's obstinacy? Perhaps Judy had met her match in the inflexible Dr. Kibbey.

We dispersed, Kei and Bradley going upstairs and I to my bedroom. Pam's note did not divulge a phone number or an address. It simply said that she would be in touch with me in the next several days. I understood that time to be alone was important for her right now. She had to let go emotionally, to undo the bonds that had tied her to Judy for more than seventeen years. She would contact me when she was ready.

The next morning I had breakfast with the family. By the time Judy seated herself at the table, Dougan had already sent Mrs. Acree's and the boys' meals upstairs in the dumbwaiter.

"I'm not ready to talk about it," Judy sounded subdued. "Don't be anxious, though. I'll be all right."

"In this I will follow your lead." I told her. "You know best."

"Planning to keep the doctor's appointment on Tuesday?" Bradley asked her. "You look so much better."

"Of course." Judy spoke serenely. "I intend to do whatever Dr.

Kibbey advises, Bradley. She is the most intelligent woman I've ever met. After all, you and Kei are perfectly capable of managing the Trilling business interests."

I choked on my coffee.

On Thursday night, Pam phoned me at The Greene Room. We made plans to meet for luncheon the next day at a sidewalk café on Colley Avenue. I arrived first and was drinking coffee when she approached our table.

"Pam, you look splendid...years younger!" I stood up to greet her. "You've weathered the storm nicely."

"And hungry as a horse, Strut. Let's order right away."

"Judy is surviving, too, but she is seeing a physician."

"Oh? She used to avoid them like the plague. Who's her doctor?"

We interrupted our conversation as our waiter approached the table. He refilled my coffee cup, poured Pam's first, and took our orders. Once he left us, I answered Pam's question.

"A Doctor Allene Kibbey. Very aloof. Mrs. Acree goes to her."

"How about that? I referred Mrs. Acree to Allene Kibbey when her previous doctor retired. Kibbey's a member of the club, Strut."

"My, my, I *had* wondered. Judy's quite impressed with her. We will see how all that goes, won't we?"

"You will, not me. I'm well out of it, I can tell you. Oh, I went through some withdrawal pangs, but not a lot. I expected to be more upset. I did my suffering *before* I moved out."

"I realize you did, and total recovery is in sight. We did worry about you, though. Not only your emotional state. Your cash flow, place of residence, new employment."

"We?"

"Derrick and I. Max has been concerned, too."

"Well, the financial situation is sound, but I do have to find an engineering job soon."

"Derrick wants to help you get a civil service position. He knows how to pull strings."

"With his help I'll be working at the Norfolk Naval Base in a month! Great! Let's go talk to him."

"This afternoon? After lunch?'

"Why not?"

The waiter brought our food and refilled our cups.

"I've taken a lease on an apartment, Strut. In the old Selden Apartments."

"Glory be! I haven't been over there since Jessie Cobb died."

"Now you'll have a good reason to visit."

"It's such a charming old building. I adore it. When do you move in?"

"First of May. Help me to furnish the apartment? I've never bought furniture before."

"Love to. I would do it up beautifully with Widdicombe family pieces we have stored on the third floor if I could smuggle them past Judy and Kei."

"Oh, why did I have to fall in love with Tidewater's most unusual lesbian?" Pam laughed. "She's so atypical."

"Yes, most gay women would insist on loaning surplus furniture, but not Judy. You and I will have to stalk the antique shops and the auctions!"

"Sounds like fun. Let's take Max along, too."

"Good thinking, Pam. He loves to go out. I took him to the Azalea Festival last week, and he had the time of his life. Now he wants me to carry him to Harborfest in June."

"I'm thankful he's doing well."

After we had eaten, I phoned Derrick, and he urged me to bring Pam to his condominium. We had drinks on his balcony and Pam was impressed with the view of the city. When they settled into discussing the possibility of a civil service position for her, I excused myself and left.

I had a four o'clock appointment with a portrait artist for my first sitting. Kei had insisted that we both have oils done of ourselves which, when finished, would visibly extend the family line hanging on the wall by the staircase at Widdicombe House. I did not look forward to the final sittings at all. I would be required to wear formal attire.

CHAPTER THIRTEEN

In early May, five days after Pam moved into the Selden Apartments, Max was hospitalized with a urinary tract infection and a temperature of 104 degrees. While a patient in Tidewater General Hospital, he began complaining of chest pains, and his breathing became slightly labored. I spent the days with him, having delegated full management of The Greene Room to Sam Zole.

On a Friday evening I returned to Widdicombe House from Max's bedside and parked in the carriage house. Hearing voices in the garden, I looked to see who was there. Judy and Dr. Kibbey were seated in white wicker chairs, drinks in their hands. Judy saw me and beckoned.

"I'll join you if you have something for me to drink," I said, walking toward them. "Today has been wretched."

"On the tea cart, dear." Judy answered. "You'll find everything you need."

Picking up a glass and the tongs, I fished three cubes from the ice bucket and dropped them in. I filled the glass half full of bourbon and then added water.

"A rather strong drink." Judy commented. "Bad day?"

"Very."

I sat opposite them and looked at Dr. Kibbey. Her brown hair was pulled back into a tight bun at the back of her neck, and her mouth formed a thin straight line. As her dark piercing eyes scrutinized me, I wondered what she was thinking.

"Take care of yourself, Mr. Widdicombe. Nothing is so dear as one's health."

"Here...in my home...I am Strut, or, at the most formal, Strutwick."

"Then you must call me Allene," she said, frowning.

"Kei is in Virginia Beach negotiating a land purchase." Judy informed us. "If it goes through, I intend to build a preplanned community with shopping center, homes, apartments, office buildings."

"Quite a large venture then," Allene commented. "Actually, I know very little about Virginia Beach."

"To me it's a resort city and a bedroom community." Judy told her. "Many people seem to prefer it."

"Glitzy." I added. "And no downtown. The beachfront is highly advertised and draws thousands of tourists. Norfolk has it's own unpublicized beach, Ocean View."

"I haven't lived here long," Allene responded, "yet I've discovered Norfolk has a nationally acclaimed museum."

"The Chrysler Museum," Judy said. "Oh, yes, one of the best. Our Virginia Opera Company is excellent, too."

"There are old families in Norfolk whose homes are not accessible, even to millionaires." I eyed the stone-faced Allene Kibbey, deciding to try shock therapy. "At the other social extreme, there are certain sections of Norfolk where one can see a fifty year old bar prostitute leaving a tavern on the strong arm of a twenty-year-old sailor."

"Oh, Strut, hush!" Judy was embarrassed.

"Simply mentioning local color." I remarked, enjoying Allene's little frown.

"I'm not offended, Judy." The doctor patted Judy's hand. "Men *are* sometimes hard to understand."

"Aren't they?" I said and got up to fix myself another drink. "In any event I prefer to live on the Chesapeake Bay, rather than on the Atlantic Ocean."

"A Widdicombe living away from Norfolk would be as strange as a fish out of water," Judy laughed.

"We did lose a few Widdicombes to North Carolina...in days gone by." I was trying to behave myself now. "It took the Yellow Fever Plague to scare them away."

"Changing the subject," Judy said, wary of the subject I had introduced, "Kei and I will be altering our social routine. Allene has persuaded me to slow down. Rather than having guests over in the evenings, we'll have business luncheons. I've already spoken to Dougan about it."

"This way they both will be able to gear down, to unwind in the evenings." Allene interjected.

"And John and Gerald are growing so fast. We'll have more time to spend with them," Judy added.

More time to spend with Allene, I thought to myself, but I smiled and said nothing. One social explanation is as good as another.

"Buffets should be appropriate." I remarked.

"Too much talk about me." Judy's expression became serious. "I want to know how Max is."

"He's to come home from the hospital on Monday, but the news is bad. Although the urinary tract infection is temporarily cleared up, there is a worse problem, a fatal one...he has lung cancer. We're not telling him, though."

"Oh, my god!" Judy groaned. "And his immune system is shut down! How awful. The last thing you needed to hear today was my prattling on."

"You diverted my mind, Judy. I am grateful for that."

"This is the employee of yours with AIDS, isn't it, Strutwick?" Allene asked.

"Yes, but much more than an employee; he is a business partner and a cherished friend."

"I don't want to seem harsh, but you may be making an error in judgment by being seen at the hospital, in his room."

"What's that?" I couldn't believe what I was hearing.

"People gossip. Even doctors do." Allene continued. "Your presence can not help this man get well, but your reputation can be tarnished. Think of your family, Strutwick."

"My reputation has been tarnished for years! After you have lived in Norfolk longer, you will realize a Widdicombe doesn't need to follow impeccable behavior."

I got up and walked back to the carriage house. Getting in my car, I drove to Derrick's. The last thing I needed was Allene Kibbey's homophobic advice. Grateful at finding Derrick alone, I embraced him.

"I can tell when you're upset, Strutwick. Tell me what's wrong."

"Unfeeling people are what's wrong, Derrick! Max is going to die, and I should not be seen visiting him, according to Dr. Kibbey!"

When I explained Max's diagnosis and Allene's cruel advice, he led me to his bedroom and soothed me. Lying in his arms on the large bed, he filled me with confidence and stamina. I treasured these moments with Derrick the most. Sex play with him was exciting, but the times like this were the true cornerstone of our love.

"We should phone Pam," he said. "She needs to know about Max."

"I will call her if you will prepare drinks for us."

"Deal," he said. We sat up, and I reached for the bedroom extension.

"Your usual bourbon and water?"

"Yes, my usual."

"You know Pam starts civil service at the base this week?"

"No, I didn't. You're marvelous, Derrick."

"I did very little. With her sterling credentials, they were eager to engage her."

During the next nine months Max underwent treatment with new drugs, some painful, and a horrible wasting away. Experimental drugs, such as Dideoxyinosine, may have helped had he taken them earlier. He could not tolerate AZT. The side effect he experienced was severe gastrointestinal problems. Large purplish lesions developed on his legs and backside. There were countless trips to physicians and clinics. He ate very little because swallowing became difficult.

Pam, Derrick, Zeke, and I took turns staying with Max who never complained. Bradley would have been there for Max, too, but I advised him to stay away. Allene Kibbey's influence over Judy was increasing. There was no need for Bradley to invite tension at home. He did call Max daily, offering encouraging words.

If I have ever known a human being that was truly pure of heart, it was Max. Watching him suffer in silence wrenched our hearts. He lost so much weight he reminded me of Holocaust victims I had seen in old newsreel footage.

By the end of February, Max was hospitalized for the last time. The moment came when the physicians advised us that he wouldn't last out the week.

One morning he looked so content when I entered his room, I wondered if he just might have a slim chance.

"Strut, I had a...wonderful dream last night!"

I sat in the chair beside his bed and stroked his arm. He was always so short of breath that I usually asked him not to talk very much; it taxed him so. This time, however, was different. The forty-three year old man was eager to relate his dream.

"I want to hear it, Max. Go slowly, though."

"Slowly is all I...can manage." He smiled up at me. "It was more like...a vision, I think. I dreamed...about Bingo. He wasn't...old and frail anymore. He was...tall and strong. It was like he was...here, in this room."

"A very good dream," I said, biting my lip.

"Bingo stood right over there...in the dream...in this room! He...was stretching out his arms to me...calling my name...over and over. And, Strut...he was grinning so...big! I felt...better than I have...in a long time."

"I like your dream, Max."

With a catch in my throat I reached for his orange juice and managed to get him to drink a little of it. Then he dozed off. Pam quietly slipped into the room. She stood behind me with her hands on my shoulders, watching Max. When he awoke, she moved to his bedside and quietly kissed him on the forehead.

"Pam, Strut, I hurt! I...need my shot!"

"Is it time?" I asked, knowing the pain medicine was administered at specified intervals.

"Past time!" He insisted, panting. "I need it now!"

Pam pushed the button to alert the nurse's station and went to stand beside the door. Because they were so busy, the nurses did not always respond immediately. Suddenly Max bolted upright in his bed, swinging one leg over the side. He began to scream with every breath.

"Don't get up!" Pam leaped to his side and tried to restrain him.

I rushed to the nurses' station and intercepted the head nurse, explaining what was happening. She prepared Max's injection, and we hurried back to his room. I was afraid; Max hadn't moved so fast in months. When we entered the room, Pam was struggling to keep him on the bed.

"Both of you hold him while I give him this shot!" The nurse directed. "And stay with him afterwards! I have to call his doctor!"

The shot brought no relief. Max cried out in pain every time he exhaled. Only because he was in such a weakened condition did we manage to keep him on the bed. A nurse's aide came in to help us. When the head nurse did return, she asked Pam and me to leave the room. The aide closed the door behind us.

"We must brace ourselves, Pam. The cancer must have reached a vital spot."

"It's so damned unfair!" Silent tears trickled down her cheeks. "There's not a sweeter soul on earth than Max. He doesn't deserve to die like this!"

"Life's not fair! You and I know that...funny, I remember telling Kei the same thing when he was eleven years old. But I believe that Max understood the unjustness of the world a long tine ago. We have to accept what life hands us and try to make the best of it."

"You brought Max happiness, Strut." Pam wiped her eyes with the corner of a handkerchief. "He was so thrilled with the Azalea Festival last year. Why, it was weeks afterwards when I talked with his, and yet he described it all so vividly to me. He was still caught up in the joy and excitement of it. Be thankful you could do that for him."

"He wanted to go to Harborfest, too." I sighed. "I wish he could have."

The nurse's aide came out of the room and told us we could go in, "He's resting now."

"What did you give him?" I asked.

"His doctor ordered morphine. He won't suffer any more."

She excused herself and hurried away. Pam and I entered the room. The nurse was arranging Max's pillows and the sheet across his lap. The head of the bed had been elevated considerably.

We went to his side and looked at him. He almost looked asleep, but I could just barely see his eyes under their drooping lids.

"'Talk to him; he can hear you," the nurse said. She was putting Max's glass, straw, and water pitcher on a tray. "And while you're here, moisten his lips from time to time with a damp cloth. Will you be staying with him?"

"Yes." I answered and moved toward the door with her. She brought the tray out with her. In the hall I asked questions.

"He has only hours now, maybe a day, at the most. Let him know that you're here and that you love him. It's all you can do."

And we did. I found a phone booth and called Derrick. He and

Zeke were at the hospital within the hour. The staff was considerate. Extra chairs were put in the room, and Zeke was sent out to buy sandwiches for our lunch.

The ex-hustler was terribly shaken by Max's impending death. Twice he had to leave the room because he broke down.

The nurses had their own speedy network that relayed Max's condition. A second-shift nurse arrived with supper for all four of us. She had cooked a pot roast with potatoes, carrots, and onions, and, when we were ready to eat that night, she heated it by the plateful in a microwave oven.

At three twenty in the morning I was holding Max's hand when he opened his eyes wide and looked at me. I smiled back. Then he trembled violently, closed his eyes, and was gone. Derrick went for the head nurse.

Max's funeral was on March 2, 1990. Pam, Derrick, Zeke, and I were seated in what would customarily be the family pew because we were the significant others. Sam Zole and five of the bartenders that had worked with Max were pall bearers. Judy, Kei, and Bradley were there; I was proud of then. Naturally Dr. Allene Kibbey was not in attendance. I was taken by surprise to see Neil Rice present. He must have been forty-eight by then, How had he known about Max's death? An attractive blond man was seated beside him. I hoped Neil was happy.

After we left the cemetery, Zeke returned to The Greene Room with Sam, and Derrick and I went to Pam's apartment for drinks.

"It's time now to start letting go, Strut." Pam advised me. "You look so worn out. Why don't you take some time off and go somewhere?"

"A little trip, perhaps? Would you go with me, Derrick?"

"Can't get away right now, Strutwick, but Pam's advice is worth considering." Derrick was sitting with his legs spread wide apart. "Why not Mexico? Should be pleasant this time of year."

"And meet some young stud south of the border? That would please you, wouldn't it?"

"No arguing this evening, Strutwick." He spoke sternly. "Let's show some respect for Max."

"I wasn't aware I was arguing!" I stood up. "Where's my coat,

Pam? I think I'll ride over to The Greene Room and give Sam some assistance."

"Sam can handle the bar," Derrick said. "Sit down and relax. It's been a rough day."

"It's been a rough day for Sam Zole, too." I shot back.

"Now, Strut," Pam interceded, "we're all three of us emotionally drained. Take it easy. Anyway, you can't leave now. I'm going to experiment on you two. At this late stage I'm learning to cook, and I have homemade cheese chowder soup. That, and sandwiches, should take care of supper."

I stayed and forced myself to be agreeable, although I was depressed. Both Max's death and the unsatisfactory state of my love life weighed heavily on my mind. A little after nine I left to drop in at the bar.

As I drove to The Greene Room, the Norfolk fog was thick and impaired visibility. I pulled into the side parking lot slowly, carefully avoiding the cars already there. After stepping out of the car and locking it, I heard footsteps that seemed to be coming toward me.

"There's one! Let's get him!" A coarse voice shouted.

I could barely make out two obscure figures through the fog. Then they were beside me.

"Wanna give me a headjob, faggot?" One of them taunted me and then pushed me backwards onto the hood of my car.

"I don't do welfare cases!" I spat the words at him.

Tales of fag-bashings flashed through my mind. I was terrified but determined not to show it. One of them grabbed me by the front of my coat and pulled me up close to him. Our faces were inches apart.

"Let go of me, you redneck trash!" I shouted.

Surprised, he loosened his grip on my coat. I lurched to the side, attempting to escape, but the second man grabbed me and twisted my arm behind my back.

"Calling us trash, huh?" he bristled. "You ought to be shot and dumped in the fuckin' bay! Show him what a real man's fist feels like, Ernie!"

The fist smashed into the side of my head.

"Help!" I cried out, hoping someone from the bar could hear me. "For god's sake, help!"

"The little queer hollers good, don't he?" The redneck laughed and drew back his fist to hit me again. "I ain't even drawn no blood yet!"

Suddenly a figure appeared out of the fog, tackling my tormentor, knocking him to the ground. They rolled on the dirt, each struggling for dominance. Surprised, the man holding my arm behind my back loosened his grip. I pushed myself backwards on him and raked my foot down his leg, stamping hard onto the bully's foot. He howled and released my arm. The other basher was on top of my rescuer, but I grabbed his head and pulled him over sideways. Now their positions were reversed, and my ally was on top.

"Get help!" he ordered me. "I can hold 'em off for now!"

He punched the man on the jaw and leaped to his feet, turning to face the other one. I ran to the bar and flung open the door, shouting to a bartender. In less than a minute I was racing back with Sam Zole and the bartender.

One attacker had fled, and my benefactor was hauling the other one to his feet, about to hit him again.

"Lemme go!" the basher pleaded as we reached them.

"Are you okay?" Sam asked my rescuer.

"Sure. Not much fight in these cowards!"

He released the man who turned to run and then kicked him on the rear. The redneck hit the ground. He scrambled to his feet and was gone in a second, swallowed by the fog.

We stood there, watching him go, catching our breaths. I turned to my rescuer.

"Saying thank you is most insufficient," I said to the stranger. "Come into The Greene Room with us, please."

We went directly into a small office off the front door, and Sam looked us over. The only damage was a bruise on my cheekbone.

"It was a glancing blow, I believe," I told them, "but are you injured, sir?'

"I'm fine. Just a little nervous, I guess," my rescuer said. "Sure could use a drink, though."

We introduced ourselves. His name was Gilford Rutledge, and he preferred to be called Gill. He was young and handsome in the boy-next-door manner, with golden-blond hair in a crew cut and light blue eyes. Those eyes communed with mine. Gill was small and compact. In the current street vernacular he would be classified as "hot."

"And I probably feel the need of libation much more than you." I responded with a smile. "Sam, both the gallant cavalier and I agree the needed remedy for our unpleasant encounter is bourbon."

"I'll fetch it," the bartender said. "This is Mr. Widdicombe, owner of the bar," he said to Gill.

"Bring glasses, a bucket of ice, and a pitcher of water with one of our best bottles of bourbon." Sam directed him, also moving toward the door.

"And a shot glass, too, please." Gill requested.

They left us, and, because the little office was overheated, we removed our coats, It was immediately obvious that the lad was well-built. Wearing a plain white tee shirt, his muscular biceps seemed almost too large for his body. He was, in essence, a miniature man.

"Please excuse me, Mr. Widdicombe. I don't mean to stare, but it's that dark red hair of yours. It's real different."

"Runs in the family." I couldn't stop looking into those blue eyes. There was a confusing blend of sincerity and sadness there.

"I'm new in town," he said, trying to carry the conversation. "Have you lived here long, sir?"

"Since 1736, and I prefer to be called Strut."

I could tell that he immediately understood my date reference. "All right. I didn't want to be pushy. You know, I enjoy hearing you talk. It's different—sort of formal but friendly."

The bartender brought our tray and put it on the desk. We were silent until he left.

"I am delighted to hear my words do not put you off, Gill. Some people feel uncomfortable in my presence because of my speech pattern."

"Well, not me. For some reason your conversation is sort of, uh...comforting."

I liked what I was hearing. Before I could drown in those blue eyes, I pulled my gaze away from them and fixed myself a bourbon and water. Gill poured himself a jigger of bourbon. Throwing his head back, he gulped it down and chased it with water.

"I see you take your bourbon neat. That's rare in someone so young."

"I guess so. I'm only twenty, but there was always liquor in the house when I was growing up."

As I sipped my drink, Gill stretched out his legs. His cuffed-up jeans were hiked above his laced-up work boots and little white socks. I could see a few inches of bare legs. They appeared to be hairless.

"If you hadn't arrived on the scene when you did, Gill, I would have been beaten badly. Seriously injured, probably."

"I'm glad I got there in time. It sure does make my first visit to a gay bar unforgettable."

"Your first visit?"

"Yep. When I went to see a movie last night, I picked up a gay newspaper in the theater lobby. They were free. Saw an ad for The Greene Room in it. That's why I came over tonight. Want to get to know some gay people like me in Norfolk. Don't know any, actually."

"Until this moment I wasn't positive you are gay."

"Sure I am. I lived with my, uh, foster brother in Richmond. He kicked me out two weeks ago."

"Your brother kicked you out? Because of your sexuality?"

"No, he liked that. I had to service him. That is, until he found a woman. He got married, so he didn't want me around any more. Gave me two hundred dollars and put me out. I decided to come to Norfolk to live on my own. He's really my fourth cousin, but we were raised like brothers."

"Have you found a job yet?"

"Oh, sure. Got a job with a landscape company right away. I live in a boarding house not too far from here."

I smiled at him in what I thought was a fatherly way. "You have achieved one thing, Gill. You have now met some 'gay people.' I, in particular, am quite delighted that you did."

"Me, too. You're special, Strut. I want to get to know you better, if you don't mind."

"I don't mind at all. The interest is mutual."

"Would it be okay if I have another shot of bourbon?"

"Feel free." I got up and poured a jiggerful of bourbon and a glass of water for him. "Are you available for dinner tomorrow night? As my guest?"

"Sure." He looked at me with those intense blue eyes. "Just don't take me to some expensive place. I don't want you to spend a lot of money on me."

"I think I can afford the dinner," I said.

Looking at the expanse of leg showing, above his jeans, I yearned to stroke it, but I had learned patience in my forty years.

CHAPTER FOURTEEN

Gill met me in front of the bar the following evening, and we drove to an Italian restaurant where we had cocktails before our chicken cacciatore. Dressed in fresh tee shirt and jeans, he apologized for not being more appropriately dressed. He said he had very few clothes. I assured him that he looked splendid. While we had an after-dinner drink, I played with his leg under the table, rubbing the toe of my shoe up and under the cuff of his jeans. He turned his blue eyes on me.

"If you keep that up, I'll be too excited to walk out of here in front of the other customers!" His voice was almost breathless. "It's been a long time since I've had any relief!"

"Help is on the way," I confided. "Am I being too forward? I don't want to scare you away."

"If you hadn't said anything, I would have." His voice was eager, and desire gleamed in his eyes. "Do you have a place where we can go?"

"I'll take you home with me, Gill. Our privacy is assured there."

"Just be gentle, please." He covered my hand with his and gripped it tightly. "I'll satisfy you, Strut. I promise."

"And I'll do likewise."

While driving to Widdicombe House, his left hand rested on my right knee. I decided to verbalize something that had been surfacing in my thoughts.

"Gill, there's one thing about you I don't understand, and I'm going to ask you about it. If the question is too personal or too painful to answer, just tell me."

"Fire away. I'll do the best I can to answer."

"I haven't known you very long, and we have had no problem in conversing. Neither of us is exactly timid. What I find strange is that you never smile. Can you tell me if I am doing or saying something I shouldn't? I do want you to feel comfortable with me."

Gill was silent. He lifted his hand from my leg and ran his fingers up and down his neck. Then he put his hand on my leg again. He was obviously uncomfortable.

"The question should not have been asked. I apologize, Gill."

"No, it's okay." He cleared his throat. "I was trying to find the right words to answer you." Again he stopped and took a breath.

"My life was great until my Uncle Don died. Then it all went downhill because I belonged to my brother, Calvin. What a mess it's been. I think my uncle's death knocked all the smiles and the laughs right out of me. I loved him very much."

"I understand." I patted his hand. "I should not have asked. You would have told me in due time."

"Strut, I do feel comfortable with you. More comfortable than I've felt with anyone in a long time."

Pulling into the carriage house, I vowed that one day Gill would smile for me. I would concentrate my efforts on it. Derrick was with Zeke so much these days. I had ample time to devote to making Gill happy, happy enough to smile radiantly.

Once in the house, we went to the kitchen where I prepared a tray of bourbon and the fixings. We carried it into my bedroom, and, locking the door, I poured him a shot.

"To cheer you," I said.

He took the jigger and downed it quickly. Foregoing his chaser of water, he stepped close to me. Again it struck me that he was quite short, for I was only five nine myself. I put my arms around his neck, running a hand through the bristles of his crew cut. He put his arms around my waist and hugged me to him. Our bodies stirred with powerful sensations as they pressed together. Then he reached up and placed a hand behind my head. Gently he stretched up to put his lips on mine. We kissed, at first chastely, but then reveling in it. My tongue probed inside his mouth, tasting his saliva, washing his teeth. When we finally released each other, both of us were panting.

"I've never been kissed like that before!" He whispered in my ear.

He moved to unbutton my shirt and remove it. I quivered as he hastily undid my trousers and, kneeling, pulled them off me. He would have begun sexual action immediately if I hadn't pulled him to his feet.

"And now you, Gill! I'm going to strip you down before the

ecstasy!"

I worked the tee shirt over his head and cast it on a chair. Then, unbuckling his Jeans, I pushed them down around his ankles. With effort I forced the pants off over his large work boots.

He was magnificent to behold. His broad chest was enriched with well-defined pectorals and from his wide shoulders hung well-developed arms. His corded stomach was flat and his hips very small, but the strength of his legs, with hard thighs and calves of rounded steel, continued down to his boots. The white socks were pushed below his shoe tops. It was a body builder's physique: compact, almost hairless, and perfectly chiseled.

We fell on the bed and indulged ourselves in hours of passion. During the night we emptied the bottle of bourbon. At dawn I took him back to his boarding house, hoping he had sufficient stamina to do a hard day's work.

After a late breakfast I drove to Derrick's condo and was relieved to find him alone. He was amiable and loving, grabbing me in his burly arms and kissing me.

"I am pleased to find you so affable today." I smiled at him before settling in a comfortable chair. "Please retain the mood throughout our discussion."

"And you, too, Strutwick." He sat on the arm of my chair. "I have something to tell you, and I don't want you flying off the handle."

"Then we both have news?" I watched him carefully and decided to let him take the lead. "You go first, Derrick."

"Remember that this has nothing to do with our love for each other. No one else can even come close to capturing my heart the way you have."

"I understand. Go on."

"Well, I'm moving Zeke into the condo today. He's—"

"Zeke is going to live with you...here?" I did not care for the concept of cohabitation.

"Easy now, Strutwick! Don't get excited. Hear me out. Zeke will be my house boy, cleaning the place, cooking breakfast, running errands. There are two bedrooms, you realize?"

"Yes, I know that." I knew my cherished private moments with Derrick would become difficult to come by. "Have you thought this through carefully?"

"Yes, I have, and I'm determined not to let it interfere with our relationship. Trust me in this. I am in love with you, but I do enjoy Zeke's young and supple body."

"How old is Zeke now?"

"He will be twenty-three in late June. why?

"Just comparing Zeke's age to that of the young man I bedded down last night. Zeke is approximately two and a half years older."

"A twenty year old man? You had sex with a twenty year old man last night?"

"Yes, and a very handsome one, too. You are correct in what you say about sleeping with young men, Derrick. They can be exciting in bed. And such staying power!"

"This is not like you at all!" He stood up and began nervously pacing the floor. "I don't think you've considered the risks involved. Diseases, that type of thing. You know how wretched AIDS can be!"

"Do not be concerned with the risk of diseases. Gill came to me directly from his cousin in Richmond, whom he serviced until the man got married."

"That is, if he's telling you the truth, Strutwick."

"I think he is. I would like some coffee, Derrick, and I believe you need some, too."

We went into the kitchen, and Derrick prepared the electric coffee maker. He was silent, and I realized he was trying to deal with the fact that I now had a young man, too.

Zeke unlocked the front door and came into the condo. He entered the kitchen and placed a bag of groceries on the counter. After we greeted him, he began putting the groceries away.

"There is more to tell, Derrick. I met Gill two nights ago when he came to my rescue."

"Ah knew uh Gill in Richmond." Zeke spoke up. "Ah usta work fer his uncle ...painting, fixing things. Ah wuz his trick, too."

"Was he small and blond?" I asked.

"Shur wuz. Uh small guy, but mighty purty. Ah guess he wuz the best looking boy ah ever seed."

"Zeke, I think we know the same young man!"

CHAPTER FIFTEEN

"Lass time ah seen Gill wuz jest aftuh his uncle's funeral. Ah had tuh fetch uh bottle uh booze fer him. He needed it bad."

"It is the same person. Gill told me he loved his uncle very much."

"He shur did. Hit fretted me tuh see him left wif that sneaky brother uh his'n. He usta push Gill around uh lot."

"What did you mean when you said this Gill needed liquor bad?" Derrick questioned Zeke. "Are you implying that he is a heavy drinker?"

"Doan know. Ah nivver seed him after dat."

"Oh, Derrick, don't find problems where there aren't any." I was defensive. "Gill needed something to drink because he was overwrought at his uncle's funeral. That is understandable. He has had drinks with me, and he handled them very well."

The coffee was brewed, so all three of us filled cups and carried them into the living room. Derrick and I sat in chairs, but Zeke stretched out on the floor at Derrick's feet. It made me uncomfortable, but Derrick always basked in the youth's adoration.

"All the same, Strutwick," Derrick warned me, "you should check it out. Being involved with an alcoholic can be unpleasant."

"That will be enough, thank you!" I insisted. "I would like to relate to you what happened to me two nights ago. After I left you and Pam. I went to The Greene Room. I was assaulted in the parking lot by two rednecks."

"Fag bashers? My god, Strutwick, are you all right? Why didn't you say something earlier?"

"I wanted to, but you were preoccupied with finding fault with Gill. I wasn't hurt, thanks to him. In fact, he came to my rescue. The only damage that was inflicted was one small bruise on my face, and it is practically gone now. You never even noticed it."

I finished my coffee and left. Conversation with Derrick had become unsatisfactory.

Gill and I continued to see each other in the evenings. I told him that I knew Zeke. Then I explained my relationship to Derrick and Derrick's to Zeke.

"Where do I fit in, Strut? If you've been in love with this Derrick for so long, then I shouldn't be falling for you like I am. You'll end up dumping me!"

"Oh, no, Gill. We Widdicombes are a strange breed. I care for you very much. My intimacy with Derrick is waning, both in verbal communication and in the bedroom. He is rather taken with Zeke now."

"Then he's a fool! You're worth a hundred Zekes!"

"Nevertheless, Derrick and I will conclude our relationship as good friends, at the very best. Our differences are not resolvable."

"I love you, Strut." Gill stretched to kiss me on the cheek. "Keep me around, please!"

"That I intend to do. I will introduce you to the family. Now that must mean my intentions are serious."

"I'll be whatever you want me to be. You call all the shots."

"Just don't grow any bigger or taller. I like your being the ultimate diminutive man! How tall are you, anyway?"

"Almost five six, but I'll grow on you."

"Figuratively speaking."

In April I invited Gill to dinner at Widdicombe House. Although he was shy and reluctant, he consented to come. The meal went well. Judy, Kei, and Bradley liked him, and the conversation flowed easily. Afterwards, Judy excused herself to visit Allene Kibbey, and Kei and Bradley left for a concert.

I gave Gill a guided tour of the house and grounds and related some of the family history to him. We ended in the library where Ross had already placed the bourbon. I mixed my drink.

"Didn't realize until tonight that you're from an aristocratic family." Gill downed a shot of bourbon and did not chase it. "I figured you were well-off because the house looked nice, what little I'd seen of it, and because you own the bar. But it's more than just being well off, Strut. You're part of the number one family in Norfolk. I wish you weren't."

"It often becomes a burden." I nodded and sipped my drink. "I was just your age when I had to assume responsibility for the entire family. We were almost bankrupt at the time."

"Rough. Did Derrick help you get on your feet?"

"I didn't know Derrick until later."

"Guess it isn't so bad now, financially I mean. But, Strut, I'll do whatever I can to help out. I'll work my balls off for you!"

Gill reached up and kissed me on the lips. I ran my fingers through his golden crew cut and fondled his hairless chest.

"By god, you are too good to be true!" I exclaimed.

"I'm one guy who won't live off you. I pay my own way. Just give me a chance to prove myself."

We had a second drink and then hastened off to my bedroom to make love. At eleven o'clock, I reluctantly dropped Gill off at his boarding house, so that the lad could sleep seven hours before going to work the next morning.

We had planned to meet at six the following evening, but I sat parked in front of his boarding house until six thirty, and he did not come out. I did not want to blow the horn. At five of seven I went to the front door and knocked. His landlady answered.

"No, he ain't gone out; he's upstairs in his room." She told me. "I went up there twice today. Once to tell him his boss called, and the other to make his bed and straighten up the room. He wouldn't come to the door either time! Had it locked."

"Perhaps he is ill," I said. "1 would like to go to his room."

"Ill? He tied one on again, that's what he done! Did the same thing his first night here. That boy can put some liquor away! Go up if you want. It's the last room at the end of the hall, third floor."

She stepped aside for me, and I went in, starting up the stairs.

"All I do is carry empty bottles out of his rooms. I'll be glad when he moves out!"

When I got to Gill's room, I knocked loudly, but there was no response. I tried the door knob; the door was locked.

"Gill!" I shouted. "Open the door! It's Strut!"

There was no answer. I hammered with my fist, calling to him. Finally I heard slow, heavy footsteps. Gill unlocked the door and, leaning on it for support, peered out. It took several seconds for his eyes to focus on me.

"Strut." his voice was slurred. "What'cha want?"

"Let me in, Gill!" I commanded. "You need help."

"Help?" He gave me a confused look. "Hey, I need sleep, man."

I pushed against the door until I could wedge myself inside. The room with one window, its shade drawn, was dark and musty. I switched on the overhead light bulb and Gill squinted his eyes. Then he weaved back to the single bed and collapsed on it, immediately closing his eyes.

I looked around the small room. Furnishings consisted of the bed, a chair, a chest of drawers, and a small, worn oval rug. Gill's jeans and tee shirt were draped over the chair, and his work boots stood neatly together in a corner. He was still wearing his little white socks and his jockey underwear.

Gill seemed to be almost in a stupor. Even so, he was a magnificent specimen of the human male. I yearned to lie beside him, to cradle his small muscular body. He needed looking after so desperately.

"Wish I could offer you a cup of black coffee." I sat on the side of the bed and stroked his derriere. "If you'll get up and dress, we can go out for some."

He rolled onto his back and gazed up at me. His eyes cleared somewhat.

"I sure did screw up this time...didn't I, Strut?" Those light blue eyes hypnotized me. "Why don't you just write me off?"

"You underestimate me, sir." I smiled at him. "What I shall do is help you to help yourself. The first step, however, is for you to come with me for coffee and something to eat."

"I don't know about the eating part...but I'll drink a gallon of coffee if you want me to." Gill sat up and moaned. "Oh, damn! I feel like hell."

By the time I got him dressed and into the car, he was trying to convince me that he had never been on so big a drunk before. I didn't debate the issue. When we entered a small café, I managed to get us a booth in the rear where we could talk privately. I plowed into my supper, but Gill didn't eat. He did gulp down several cups of coffee. Finally he seemed alert.

"Should we contact your employer? I don't want him to terminate you."

"I have his home number on me. I'll call him when we leave."

"Gill, we have to be honest with each other if we are going to develop a strong relationship. You understand that, don't you?"

HOUSE OF BROKEN DREAMS 147

"Sure," he said, "but I'll never get wiped out like that again! I promise."

"I know you are convinced you won't, Gill. At this moment, that is." I put my hand over his. "Later can be different. You will likely yield to temptation then."

"I need you, Strut! I need you so much!" His eyes were pleading, undeniable.

"And I need you. Believe that. We all have our crosses to bear, and sometimes they can become incredibly burdensome. First, let me say that your landlady tattled on you."

"What?"

"She told me that you got snockered your first night in her house, that you drink on a regular basis, and...that she wants you out of her house."

"I *have* to have the liquor." Gill lowered his head, and his hand trembled under mine. "I've never told that to anybody before in my life, except Calvin...my cousin. And he knew it anyway!"

"That is precisely *why* you can't stop drinking on your own. I want you to go to AA, and I'll invest all the emotional support and love and patience that you will need."

"Oh. I don't know, Strut." He sagged, his eyes downcast.

The waitress stopped at our booth to refill his coffee cup. He pulled his hand away from mine and jerkily wiped his forehead. When she was gone, I continued.

"You don't have to be alone in this. I am prepared to move you into Widdicombe House. Alone is when you succumb to the devil's brew, isn't it?" I smiled at my use of the antiquated expression.

"Well, yes, it is, but AA rules wouldn't let me have anything to drink, not even a swallow!"

"You can do it," I rubbed my foot against his leg. "I will also abstain. I don't have to have it."

"You will? You'd give up your bourbon for me?"

"And my wine and my beer and my egg nog at Christmas ...gladly."

I wouldn't know how to act, living in your house." He was loosening up now, "I haven't lived with kindly people since my Uncle Don died."

"Acting naturally is all you need do. Kei and Judy already like you. There's a room waiting for you on the third floor. It hasn't been occupied in years. Since Mrs. O'Brian, our housekeeper, retired."

He grabbed my hand with both of his and pulled it to his face, kissing it.

"I'm grateful, Strut. I really am."

"The nights when you are tortured by your thirst, and there will be such nights, you will stay in my room. We will endure the bad moments together."

"I'll give it everything I've got." A silent tear slipped down each cheek. "Nobody's given a damn about me for the last two years. Nobody until I met you. I'll make it, Strut. I know I will! You won't be sorry."

As we left the café, Gill used the phone booth just outside to call his employer. The man administered a tongue-lashing, but Gill still had his job.

We went by the boarding house where Gill picked up his clothes in two brown paper bags and turned in his key. At Widdicombe House we found Dougan still in his kitchen. I explained that Gill would be living with us, residing in Mrs. O'Brian's old room.

"Sounds like Ross and I have a neighbor now up top. That's good. Glad to have you aboard, Gill."

They shook hands and Dougan offered us something to eat. I declined, but Gill did not.

"Maybe I can eat something now, if it's okay, Strut. I think I'll sleep better if I do."

"Enjoy. I shall speak to Kei while Dougan tempts you with his delicious cooking."

I left Gill in the kitchen and ran into Kei coming down the stairs. we went into the library.

"Gill is moving in. I am putting him on the third floor. He is to live with us. Please don't challenge me on this, Kei."

"I won't, however, I wonder if it is wise. Gill is eleven years younger than even I am. Do you think he will be faithful to you?"

"I am sure of that. He is devoted to me, and, what's more, he needs me."

"That handsome young man needs you? Be realistic, Strut."

"He has a drinking problem, and I am going to help him to overcome it. I want you and Judy to know so that neither of you will offer him a drink. I will also discreetly alert Dougan and Ross. And further, none of our food will be prepared with cooking wine.

"You're going to help Gill beat his alcohol problem? You like your drinks yourself."

"I am giving it up, giving up all alcoholic beverages. Gill intends to go to AA. There's one in walking distance, and I shall call them in the morning."

"All right, Strut. Judy and I won't oppose you. Give it your best shot. I hope Gill succeeds."

The next morning, after inquiring into the times of the AA chapter's meetings, I phoned Derrick and told him everything. I refused to ever be less than totally honest with him. Derrick was still very much at the center of my heart.

"I'm not trying to discourage you, Strutwick, but bringing that young man into your home is a mistake. Let him live upstairs over The Greene Room, in Max's large room."

"Live near all that beer and liquor? No thanks, Derrick. No one could withstand that temptation every night."

"There's alcohol in Widdicombe House, too,"

"I will keep the liquor cabinet here in the library locked. Give Kei and Judy keys. All the rest goes out of the house."

"Gill is an alcoholic. He has probably never tried to do without."

"He is trying now with all his heart and soul. He needs to be around people, and he will be...at work, here, and at AA."

"AA be damned! Gill is flawed, seriously flawed!"

CHAPTER SIXTEEN

The rest of April was a roller coaster with Gill experiencing peaks and valleys. There were nights we lay together in my double bed as I held the trembling young man in my arms. Never phoning his AA contact, he relied totally on me for emotional support.

Derrick apologized to me for his pessimistic outburst, and a week later, on a Saturday afternoon, invited us over for coffee. He and I watched in wonder as Gill and Zeke embraced with affection and told each other what had happened in their lives since they had last seen each other in Richmond. The two of them were a study in blond glory. Five foot six, golden haired Gill was so serious, his light blue eyes shining, and towheaded Zeke, about three inches taller, alternately grinned and frowned as he listened, his green eyes full of expression. My first sight of the two of them together etched a living portrait in my mind. I had never before been in the company of two such marvelous specimens of male beauty.

We settled in the living room of the condominium and Zeke served us cake and coffee. Derrick congratulated Gill on his excellent beginning in abstinence.

"Well, I've got Strut's support. Couldn't do it without him," Gill said.

"But yore doing hit," Zeke grinned. "Ah saiz yuh got uh lot uh will powuh."

"And he hands money over to Judy each Friday. To cover his meals and lodging." I was proud of Gill. "He insisted on doing it."

"Gill, I understand now that you are good for Strut," Derrick said, "He and I are on better terms than we've been in a long time. Not fighting any longer, thanks to you."

When we left Derrick's, I took Gill shopping. Although he was reluctant to accept them, I bought him a bathrobe and some sports clothes. Between paying Judy for his keep and buying needed work clothes, he had little more than lunch money left over from his minimum wages.

Weeks passed, and Gill remained on the wagon. His self-confidence strengthened as he remained sober. My own abstaining was not without some effort, too. It gave me a small sample of Gill's sacrifice.

In early June Pam phoned. I immediately detected a restrained joy in her voice.

"I've met someone, Strut. Maybe I shouldn't get excited yet, but I had to tell you."

"Ah, the first bright spot in my summer!" I was pleased. "Tell me about her, Pam."

"Her name's Karen, and I met her on the base. She's Civil service, a secretary, been there for years. It's too soon to tell, but we get along just great."

"What do you mean, too soon? If your heart says yes, then full steam ahead!"

"Oh, you know how we lesbians are! We need time. Besides, Judy is the only woman I've ever been in love with. That was my only relationship. I need to go slowly with this new possibility. And Karen agrees."

"Why Karen?"

"She's a late bloomer. Divorced a year and a half ago. No children, though. I'm thankful for that."

"When do I get an introduction? I promise to be on my best behavior."

"Saturday night, if you agree. I want you to come for supper. I'm fixing pot roast, all the vegetables self-contained in one pot, so I don't think it will be too difficult. I love learning to cook."

"You will manage adroitly, my dear. But I do have an important request." I explained the situation with Gill, expressing my interest in him, although Pam did not understand how I continued my connection with Derrick.

Explaining that the romantic rectangle was strange for all four of us, I emphasized that it was working. Derrick and I no longer quarreled, and we treasured more than before our quality time together. Then I plunged into Gill's alcoholism and described his need to avoid temptations to indulge.

"No problem, Strut. We won't have any alcoholic beverages in sight. Karen lives with a lesbian couple, and I know they don't drink. By the way, Derrick and Zeke are also coming."

After we hung up, I thought about Pam and all she had endured with Judy who, in contrast, had not required a long interim between lovers. I did not know anyone who deserved to achieve personal happiness more than Pam.

When Gill and I arrived at the Selden Apartments on Saturday evening, Derrick, Zeke, Karen, and the other women were already there. I was mighty proud of Gill who resembled a male model in his blue knit sport shirt, white duck pants, and sockless tennis shoes. Introductions were made, and we mixed in a congenial manner.

I liked Karen immediately. She was a tall woman, about the age of Pam and myself, with long brown hair and brown eyes. There was sincerity in her expression and in her manner. Moreover, she seemed to dote on Pam. The prospects of a coupling appeared to be promising.

After dinner the group sat in the living room, talking and drinking coffee or Coke. Gill sat beside me, needing the closeness.

"Say, I almost forgot," Derrick began, "that I brought along a little surprise for you people." He jumped up and started for the kitchen. "Hold up on that coffee. You're going to like this!"

He returned with a dark brown bottle that had to be a type of liquor. As he placed it on the coffee table, I bristled.

"This is a delicacy, people. It's all chilled and goes well with your coffee, too."

"I'll get glasses," Karen said, rising and going to the kitchen.

"I don't think you should offer it at this time, Derrick." I stared at him menacingly. "Some of us present do not imbibe!"

"Relax, Strutwick, this is not whiskey. It's only an after-dinner drink. Couldn't be a problem for anyone."

"What is it?" Pam asked, looking doubtful.

"It's Dartleys Original Irish Cream Liqueur, and there's hardly any alcohol in it at all. It's been around for a while, but I've just discovered it.

"Derrick's got 'bout twenty-five mo' bottles of hit at home. Ah knows, cuz ah toted um home fer him." Zeke announced happily. "Hit duz taste mighty fine."

"None for me, thank you," I said, as Karen arrived with a tray of glasses. "Skip me, too." Gill added, eyeing the bottle intently. Derrick poured the creamy liquid in six glasses and passed them to the rest of the group. One of the women sipped hers, then set the glass on the coffee table and pushed it away. Her lover followed suit.

"It does contain alcohol." She spoke firmly. "I'm certain of that."

Pam looked uncomfortable as she tasted the liqueur that had been placed before her. It was obvious that Karen had no knowledge of Gill's alcoholism; she was only aware of the fact that her sharemates did not drink.

"It's marvelous!" Karen smiled. "Why haven't I tried this before?"

"That's what I said, Karen," Derrick answered and then turned to Gill. "You *should* taste it. There's very little alcohol content, and it tastes terrific. Like a very rich cream, but sweet, too."

"No, thanks." Gill's calm expression belied the desperation I saw in his eyes. "I'll stick to my Coke."

I was proud of Gill and told him so as we drove home.

"Have to get a firm handle on my drinking problem, Strut." Gill looked at me adoringly. "I can't let you down."

"And you won't." I patted his knee. "You are developing pride in yourself now...possibly for the first time in years. Isn't that true?"

"It sure is. My Uncle Don made me feel good about myself, but nobody else did, 'til I met you."

We parked the car in the carriage house and went to my bedroom. Building self-esteem in Gill was essential, and I did it sincerely.

"Zeke turns twenty-three near the end of the month. I'm positive Derrick will have a party for him. There will be drinking."

"So I'll handle it." Gill stated. "It's only early June now. Why, I've got almost the whole month to practice saying no."

"You are magnificent, Gill. And very, very dear to me."

Then it happened. The corners of Gill's mouth slowly turned up until he was grinning broadly. I was astonished.

"I can't believe this!" I exclaimed. "Do you know what's happening, Gill?"

His mouth opened, and his face became illuminated in a beautiful smile. His even white teeth flashed, and his blue eyes radiated happiness.

"You said I'm 'very, very dear' to you!" Gill grabbed me and hugged me close. "Now I *know* everything's just great in my world!"

He washed my face and neck with wet kisses. When his strong arms did release me, I was panting.

"I should have said those words sooner. I've felt them in my heart for some time."

"Don't ever stop saying them, Strut! I'll never get tired of hearing them! I'm yours, all yours."

I dropped across my bed and looked up at my muscular young man. At that moment I knew that Gill was all I needed to make me perfectly happy. In some magical way he had dispelled my emotional need for Derrick. Gill came to lie beside me. He was all I would ever want in a man. I knew this now as well as I knew my name.

"We owe ourselves a little celebration, I believe. Why don't we take the Spirit of Norfolk cruise next weekend?"

"Sounds good to me." Gill ran his hand inside my shirt and lightly stroked my chest. "What is the 'Spirit of Norfolk,' anyway?"

"A cruise ship. It's fun. It makes daily excursions through the waterways of Hampton Roads. Has an excellent buffet, too."

"Ah, that's nice. I'd like it. Can I kiss you on the deck?"

"I don't believe Tidewater, Virginia is quite ready for that, but I've seen the time I would do it...when I was your age. Just do not dare me, sir!"

The next afternoon we received distressing news at Widdicombe House. Mrs. O'Brian's sister phoned from Bowling Green to inform us that, at seventy-nine, the dear woman had died in her sleep. Kei, Judy, and I were genuinely saddened. The funeral was set for Tuesday morning. There was never the remotest thought of our not going. Mrs. O'Brian had occupied a very special place in our lives, especially mine.

Within the hour I had reached Pam. She, too, wanted to attend the funeral. I wondered if she and Judy should be brought together, even under these circumstances.

"I think Judy and I can manage to be civil to each other...for Mrs. O'Brian's sake. We both loved her very much."

"Kei and I thought it would be preferable to drive up tomorrow and spend the night because the funeral is Tuesday morning. If we spent the night in the vicinity, we would be rested the next morning."

"Then I'll go up tomorrow, too. I have some time accumulated at work. It amounts to vacation time. I want to be there," Pam said.

"We will take two cars, and you shall ride with me. Bowling Green is near the interstate; I am confident there is a choice of motels in the area," I said.

"Oh, yes. You and I can stay in a separate motel from the others."

"That should be acceptable to Judy. I'll inform her that you are going, Pam."

Later I called a family conference, and we met in the drawing room. Gill and Bradley were also present. Judy readily accepted the news that Pam was going to the funeral. They would not be in each other's presence except at the church and the graveyard.

We decided we would leave at one o'clock the next day. Bradley surprised us by stating that he would not be going, but Gill seemed to like the idea that he would not be left entirely alone.

"You and I can spend some time together," Gill told Bradley. "Make sure I don't stray from the straight and narrow path!"

"I'd like that," Bradley said. "Let's go out for dinner...seafood, maybe? No sense in Dougan preparing a big meal for just the two of us."

After the family disbanded, Gill and I met in my room to discuss my impending absence.

"Don't worry about me, Strut. I'm self-reliant now. I won't even be tempted to have a drink."

"Well, Bradley can be your insurance policy. He is good company, and you won't even think of indulging."

"Being without you tomorrow night will be the tough part," Gill said. "I'll miss you so much."

"I shall suffer that loss, too."

That evening I called Derrick to let him know that Mrs. O'Brian had passed away. He was his usual comforting self, offering to make the trip with me.

"Your offer is appreciated, but I am self-sufficient now. It is, by the way, a good feeling."

"What do you mean, Strutwick? Mrs. O'Brian mothered you when you were a baby. She was a central figure in your life for years. You may be surprised at the emotion you'll feel once the funeral is underway."

"The thought that Gill is here waiting for me...in my house...will sustain me."

"Is Gill the reason you rarely see me anymore?"

"Frankly, yes, Derrick. I've pledged myself to him." There was a long pause.

"I want you to think this over, Strutwick. Don't make a hasty decision."

"The fellow is completely devoted to me, as Zeke is to you. We are both fortunate."

Derrick continued to try to persuade me to postpone breaking off with him until we could sit down together and talk about it. I resisted, and finally he hung up on me.

The trip to Bowling Green went smoothly. I was surprised at how much Mrs. O'Brian's sister resembled her. Steeling myself, I endured the sorrow of the funeral service and silently bade farewell to my beloved Mrs. O'Brian. As had been expected, Judy and Pam saw each other only at the ceremony and the burial. If either had any difficulty with the other's presence, neither displayed it.

Returning, Pam and I drove into Norfolk via the Hampton Roads tunnel, and I dropped her at the Selden Apartments. When I reached Widdicombe House, Kei and Judy had not yet arrived. I walked into the house, and Dougan came quickly to meet me.

"Get ready for trouble, Strut," he warned me. "Gill got roaring drunk last night! Broke into the liquor cabinet in the library and did his damnedest to drink it dry!"

"Where's Bradley?" I charged into the hall, Dougan following at my heels. "Is he home yet?"

"He never went in today. Been trying to find Gill Rutledge."

"Gill's gone?" I felt a pang of terror. "Where?"

Just then Bradley came out of the library. He stared at me and held his hands out, palms upward, in despair.

"Tell me what happened, Bradley." I felt numb. "Why did Gill start drinking?"

Bradley related what he knew, which was most of the scenario. He and Gill never had gone out for dinner together last night as they had intended. Shortly after Gill came in from work, Derrick and Zeke came by and convinced Gill to go to the condo for dinner.

Bradley was invited, too, but had declined, knowing Kei would not approve. Gill returned to Widdicombe House alone after midnight...intoxicated.

He went to Bradley and demanded a key to the liquor cabinet. When Bradley refused, Gill broke it open with a hammer and screw driver. He proceeded to drink himself into a stupor while Bradley pleaded with him to stop. Finally Gill passed out in the kitchen. Ross put a blanket over him.

By that time it was three thirty in the morning. Bradley, Ross, and Dougan went to bed, thinking Gill would be sober after having slept. At eight o'clock Dougan came downstairs, and Gill was gone. He roused Bradley who began searching for Gill, by car and by phone. The search had been fruitless.

"I've called his job, and I've called Derrick," Bradley moaned. "I would have checked the boarding house where he used to live, but I don't know where it is."

"Derrick is behind this!" I was incensed. "He tempted Gill to drink! I know he did! He tried once before!"

CHAPTER SEVENTEEN

When Kei and Judy arrived, Bradley repeated the circumstances of Gill's disgrace.

"I tried to tell you that Gill wouldn't work out, Strut, but you wouldn't listen." Kei was not sympathetic. "Now, for god's sake, put the man out of your mind."

"I intend to find him...help him sober up," I fired back, "and I do not give a tinker's damn whether you like it or not, Kei."

"I won't have him living here again." Kei spoke sternly. "That's final."

"No ultimatums. Both of our names are on the deed to this house!"

"An alcoholic will steal to get money for whiskey," Dougan said. "I had an uncle like that."

"Does Gill have a key to the house?" Judy worried. "I won't feel safe nights if he does."

"He may come back for his clothes," Kei wondered aloud. "At any time of the day or night...when we're all sleeping!"

"While Gill was drinking, he kept saying that he was no good, not worthy of you, Strut," Bradley told me. "I couldn't stop him from drinking, but I felt so sorry for him."

"Thank you, Bradley," I said. "You are the only one here with a heart."

"That's not true, Strut." Judy countered. "We are concerned for the family, for Widdicombe House. And there are John and Gerald to be considered, too. Have you thought about what effect all this can have on their young lives? Having a drunk in the house?"

"I'll speak to Mrs. Acree, alert her to the problem." Kei soothed Judy. "She's a resourceful woman and will take precautions."

I turned and walked away from them. They disgusted me. Bradley was the only one among then who had an ounce of compassion. Shutting myself up in the library, I dialed Sam Zole's home number; he was still living with his lover in East Ocean View. Sam suggested I offer a cash reward to whomever could help us locate Gill. Between the two of us we contacted the owners of the other gay bars in Tidewater, giving each of them a description of Gill and both Sam's and my phone numbers, as well as the number of The Greene Room. Then Sam called Gill's employer and made the same offer while I drove over to Gill's boarding house to tempt his ex-landlady. She was greedily interested in winning the reward money and promised to check with the other keepers of boarding houses she knew.

I did not want to talk to Derrick, so Sam took it upon himself to call the man whom I believed was responsible for the dilemma. Derrick pledged his cooperation.

With nothing more to be done for the moment, I went to the kitchen of Widdicombe House, a bottle of bourbon in hand, and made myself a drink. It was my first since the evening Gill and I had mutually agreed to abstain. I needed it. Even though I felt that Gill would be found, I was emotionally drained.

Perhaps when Gill was located, I could convince him to commit himself to a resident center for the treatment of alcoholism. There he could be dried out under supervision, and I would visit him regularly until the day he could be released. My loving support was not sufficient. Gill also needed professional help.

Days evolved into weeks, and my optimism faded. Sam called Derrick twice a week because I refused to talk to my ex-lover. However, in fairness to him, I did not think he was withholding any information as to Gill's whereabouts. Derrick understood the gravity of the situation and realized he would have absolutely nothing to gain by lying.

Depression burdened me so that I often sat in the library, its sliding doors closed, and stared at the four walls, How could I accept the loss and the downfall of sweet, handsome Gill? When I closed my eyes, I envisioned his first smile, a smile filled with trust and love. I ached to have his hard muscular body press against me. At age forty I had found this splendid young man, but he had been snatched from me by alcohol addiction.

Had he left the Tidewater area? The thought terrorized me. I wondered if he had returned to Richmond. Perhaps a trip to the capital city was the answer. Gill may have gone back to his foster brother's house. I thought his name was Calvin, and they had the same surname, Rutledge. With a Richmond city directory, I decided I could locate the house.

Before I could call Sam to relate my plan, he phoned me. It was late Saturday morning when I picked up the telephone in the library.

"Strut, I think I saw Gill last night as I was driving home from The Greene Room. Actually it was early this morning, about two thirty."

"Oh, thank heaven! Is he all right, Sam?"

"Don't know about that. He wasn't in a very savory environment. What's the name you and Max used to call East Ocean View Avenue? The Street of Broken Dreams?"

"Yes, that's it. Because of the drugs, booze, bars, and street hustlers out there."

"Well, that's where I saw him. At least I think it was Gill. Sure looked like his blond hair to me. He was walking slowly down the Street, staring at the passing cars, the way hustlers do. My car lights were on him for only a few seconds, but I believe it was our boy."

"Hustling on the Street?"

"Appeared to be, but who knows? Want to take a look tonight...the two of us?"

"Definitely, Sam. And perhaps we could start cruising the Street earlier. Do you have a reliable assistant manager we can leave in charge of the bar tonight? One who can handle the money?"

"Oh, sure, two, a man and a woman. No problem. We'd best go in my car, though, If it is Gill, he will recognize your car right off."

I thanked Sam and we ended our conversation. Sitting there in the library, I decided the spacious room looked bleak. Oak bookcases reached to the ceiling on two sides, filled with books that appeared too formal, almost forbidding. No life here. The leather arm chairs loomed dark and depressing. No life at all.

What was wrong with me? This was the same room I had adored for years, and now it seemed somber and strange. Tension and depression, that had to be it. I was not myself, hadn't been since Gill left. I wanted him more than anything in the world. More than money, family prestige, more than Widdicombe House itself. He had wrapped himself around my heart in such a short time. I had to have Gill back...even if he drank. Time spent in his presence was what mattered most. I loved him more than I had any of the others: Vic, Neil, or Derrick. I refused to face life without him.

I met Sam at The Greene Room at eleven thirty, and we were cruising the Street of Broken Dreams before midnight. Cars blasted their radios and their horns and they shot around us in the left lane. Other automobiles poked along as slowly as we did, cruising the sidewalks for pickups. Noise and music blared from bars as sailors, civilians, and bar sluts streamed in and out of their doors, frantic and boisterous in their revelry. I wondered if Sam and I were the only sober people on the Street.

Just ahead of us, one car sideswiped another. They pulled over and the drivers leaped out. Sam stopped until he could get around them. When we did pass, the two drivers were arguing and cursing in the Street.

Male and female hustlers stared at us when we drove by them. I was too anxious to find Gill. My nerves were raw and edgy. Not one of the men on the Street resembled Gill in the least.

When we completed the run, Sam turned the automobile around and started back. A police car was in the parking lot of a bar, and I spotted two uniformed officers in the midst of a small but excited crowd. "Probably breaking up a fight," Sam commented.

"Gill doesn't belong out here," I said. "He won't survive in this element."

Our return run wasn't successful either. Sam carefully repeated the circuit, and then we stopped in an all-night convenience store for coffee. Back in the car I sipped mine and sighed deeply.

"I think it's hopeless, Sam."

"We're not about to give up yet. The hard core hustlers are hitting the streets just about now. Our chances of finding Gill will improve every minute."

"You do think he is into hustling then?"

Sam paused before answering me. He stared intently into my eyes. "Yes, I definitely felt that last night, Strut."

When Sam's coffee cup was half empty, he placed it in a cup holder and began again to patrol the Street. On the fourth run we spotted a lone figure walking slowly down the Street, weaving a little, and watching the cars. Sam slowed down to a crawl.

"That's him, Sam! I recognize the clothes! He's blond, too!" I cried.

"Now stay cool, Strut. I'm going to pass him, real slow. You wedge down in the seat so he'll think I'm alone."

I did as he said and slid down on the floor. Sam passed the man, managing to flash a smile, made a right turn at the corner, and stopped. He turned off the car's lights and we waited. The side street was quieter; I heard slow footsteps approaching,

"Need a lift home, friend?" Sam called out. Then to me he whispered, "Sit up quick, Strut, so he'll recognize you!"

I sat up and spotted Gill coming toward the car. He was only yards away.

"Hey, there's two of you!" Gill slurred his words. "What kind of funny stuff you guys up to?"

"It's me...Strut! Come here, please!"

Gill focused his eyes on me with effort, but I knew he had recognized my voice. He stood still and stared.

"Get outta here!" he yelled. "Leave me alone!"

Then he turned and weaved back toward the Street. I jumped out of the car and ran after him.

"Strut, no!" Sam yelled.

I caught Gill's arm as he reached the street. He tried to shrug me off, but I hung on to him.

"I'll help you, Gill! Come back with me! I'll get you professional help!"

Out of the corner of my eye I could see Sam running toward us. The traffic was heavy, and the headlights partially blinded me.

"Don't you see? Turn me loose!" Gill swayed as he stood there staring at me. "I love liquor better'n anything else! And I can always earn money to buy it out here!"

"I love you so much!" I implored.

His eyes cleared, and I saw pain there. Then he jerked his arm free. Running crookedly, he fled up the Street, and I ran after him. Sam was following behind me. Gill veered to his left and ran into the traffic.

A car in the right lane slammed on his brakes to avoid hitting him, but a red pickup truck in the left lane struck Gill, spinning him crazily into the air. I watched from the curb in horror. Gill smashed to the pavement, his right leg twisted under him grotesquely. I could hear a woman near me screaming, and then Sam was there, restraining me. All traffic stopped.

"Let go of me!" I was hysterical. "I've got to get to him! Damnit, let go!

"I'll call the police!" The woman that had screamed was yelling. "There's a phone in this motel!"

She ran into the building, and the two sailors who had been with her stayed with us.

"You stay here, Strut, and I'll go see how bad it is!" Sam urged. "Don't get involved! It can't help!"

"I don't care about anything but Gill!" I was shouting hoarsely, trying to break free. Sam turned to the two sailors who were watching us.

"My friend's out of his head! Will you keep him here while I go out there? He can't help, and he's about to fall apart as it is!"

"Sure," one sailor said, taking me firmly by the arm. "You go see if there's anything you can do."

"I got the pick-up's licence number," the other sailor volunteered, as he fished a pencil out of his pocket. "They'll nail that bastard for hit-and-run driving! Go! We'll keep your buddy here."

Sam worked his way through the gathering crowd. I could barely see him kneel down by Gill. Then the people closed in and obstructed my view. The woman came back to us.

"I don't believe this! It isn't real!" I moaned, shaking my head.

"Don't you worry, honey!" The woman tried to comfort me. "The police are coming! The medics, too!"

I tried to break loose from the sailor's grip, but he held me fast. A lifetime passed before Sam came back. As he reached me, the medics and the police were arriving.

"Tell me! Tell me, Sam!" I implored.

He shook his head slowly and then looked at the sailors.

"Will you guys help me get him in the car? There's nothing he can do here. I want to take him home."

Once Sam and I were inside his automobile, the sailors stood by my closed passenger door until we drove away. I buried my head in my hands in despair. Neither of us talked until the car stopped in front of Widdicombe House.

I could not cry. It would have helped so much if I had been able to cry. Life had staggered me too many times. Young Gill Rutledge, though only twenty, had been buffeted about, too, but his problems were behind him now. We had shared happiness, but it had been snatched from us. There was no meaning in anything left for me. Nothing in the future mattered.

"Go inside and rest, Strut. It's over, and we can't do anything about it."

"Tell me about it, Sam." I turned and looked him in the eye. "Every detail. I must have that."

"No, I can't. It won't help now." He shook his head, staring blindly at the dashboard.

"If you ever had any regard for me at anytime, you will do it."

"Strut, you know I'm your friend. Don't talk like that." The dim lights from the dashboard left most of his face in shadow.

"Then give me what I need! Gill's last moments! I have to have the memory! Don't try to shield me!"

"It would he cruel to describe it to you."

"If you don't," I said slowly, "I shall go mad. I have so little to remember Gill by. For god's sake, give me his death!" I clutched his arm in my grief.

"All right, Strut, but I don't want to."

"Omit nothing!"

"When I reached Gill, I knew right away that he was all smashed up...broken bones, internal injuries. Blood was coming from his mouth and nose and ears. He was dying. I spoke to him, told him who I was. I took his hand and held it, but he probably didn't even know that. His eyes sort of fastened on me, and I saw a flicker of recognition in them. Then he spoke in such a weak voice that I had to bend close and strain to hear him. Gill said, 'I shouldn't have run away. Tell Strut I love him.' Talking took even more out of him. His eyes closed and he shook all over. Then he relaxed and died. I could almost see the life leave his body."

"Are you leaving out anything? Anything at all?"

"No. When I knew he was gone, I left him and came back to you."

"Thank you, Sam. Never feel that you did the wrong thing in telling me. Even though you spoke of Gill's agony, you did the essential thing. I have to have the memory."

"Go rest now, Strut. I'll call you tomorrow."

I patted him on the hand and opened the car door. Moments later I was in my bedroom. "Paradise Lost," I said out aloud, comprehending totally what hopelessness truly was. Max was infinitely correct. That hell-hole was aptly named the Street of Broken Dreams.

CHAPTER EIGHTEEN

I undressed and put on my bathrobe. Fleetingly I thought of Pam and her budding relationship with Karen. It could work. No one is ever guaranteed happiness, but I wanted Pam to find it. She was such a giving person. More deserving than anybody I knew.

Not like Derrick, who was responsible for Gill's death. Derrick had tempted him to drink; I would make him admit it. Gill was sober when Derrick had taken him to the condominium, and Gill was drunk when he returned. It was simple to deduce what had happened.

Derrick did not know that Gill was dead, and the accident had occurred too late to be reported in the morning newspaper. I would go to the condo about nine o'clock. It would pleasure me to place this burden on Derrick. I intended for him to feel fully accountable. He would carry the millstone around his neck for the remainder of his life. This would indeed be a confrontation.

Afterwards I would retreat to Widdicombe House and remain here. It would become my refuge, my sanctuary. Nothing remained for me elsewhere.

My temples were throbbing. Going to the powder room, I took two aspirins. As I looked at my reflection in the mirror, I realized I hadn't shaved at all Saturday. Now the stubble looked slovenly. There were dark circles under my bloodshot eyes. My looks were gone; I would never again be an object of desire to any gay man. It made no difference. I was finished with love or lust or whatever it was.

At daybreak my head still pounded. I pulled on some dirty clothes and left the house, The car was not needed. I walked downtown. How strange the commercial district appeared. It resembled a stage set, hours before the play was scheduled to commence. I passed Neil's old office; it was a magazine shop now.

I don't know how long I roamed aimlessly. Seeing the high-rise building where Derrick lived, I quickened my pace. I looked to the top at his condominium. No lights were on. How like Derrick to

HOUSE OF BROKEN DREAMS

buy a unit on the top floor.

I entered a small restaurant across the street from Derrick's building and sat at a table up front, next to the plate glass. From there I could see Derrick's windows if I bent my head slightly. I drank only black coffee, repeatedly searching for a light in the windows. Checking my key chain, I knew I still retained a key to Derrick's front door. Access would be easy.

My head ached. Once I had confronted Derrick, I would go home and sleep. Rest would take care of the throbbing.

Lights finally came on in the condo. I smiled, knowing Derrick's routine so well. Ordering yet another cup of coffee, I watched the building carefully. An hour passed, and then I saw Zeke leave through the front door. I rose, paid for my coffees, and left.

Crossing the street I walked casually into the building through a side door and took the elevator to the top floor. Surprised not to encounter any of the inhabitants, I decided that it was still too early for these yuppies to be up and about. I put my key in the door and unlocked it.

Derrick was not in the living room. For a moment I wondered if he had left undetected by me. Then I saw him. He was on the balcony, a glass in his hand. Crossing to the glass door, I opened it and stepped outside. He was startled.

"Strutwick! I didn't hear you come in. What the devil are you doing here this early?'

"Not to bring you glad tidings." I stared at him. He was wearing only his bathrobe. I knew there was nothing under it. "The news is grave."

"Have some orange juice with me? Or some coffee? There's still coffee in the kitchen. My god, Strutwick, you look terrible!"

"I have been up all night," I said tonelessly. "I hope you slept peacefully."

"It's not like you to be so unkempt. Tell me what has undone you."

He walked to the end of the balcony and leaned against the railing. "Gill died early this morning. Struck down by a hit and run driver. I saw it happen." There was no emotion in my voice.

"Oh. my god! No wonder you look so defeated! I'll take care of you, Strutwick. I'll be at your side through this." Those words struck a bell in my memory. Who was it—Vic?—who had said those words to me once before?

Derrick came to me and put his hands on my shoulders.

"Release me!" I shouted at him. "I don't want you to touch me...ever again!"

He dropped his hands and went back to lean on the railing.

"You are not yourself, Strutwick." He seemed to be avoiding my eyes. "Why don't you stretch out on my bed and rest? A man can take only so much!"

"I was never so completely myself, Derrick, as I am at this moment." I spoke very slowly. "And I will not lie on your bed. Your bed is too crowded!"

He stared at me for a moment and apparently decided not to pursue the subject. "Gill...do they know who did it?"

"Not sure, but I do."

"You aren't making sense!" Derrick stared at me strangely.

"*You* murdered Gill just as surely as if you had pushed him in front of that truck!" My rage surfaced again. "I know that you brought him over here the day he fell off the wagon! I know he came home intoxicated!"

"Hell, Strutwick, all he had here was some Bartleys Irish Cream! The stuff is hardly alcoholic! Don't blame me! The kid was an alcoholic!"

"Bartleys or grain alcohol, it doesn't make any difference!" I stepped toward him until my face was close to his. "You started him drinking again! Accept your guilt, Derrick!"

"When you do get your self-control back, you will see all this differently. For right now, know that I love you."

Derrick leaned back on the railing. Quickly I brought my arms up and straight-armed him in the chest, pushing against him with all the delirious strength in ne. He shot me an incredulous look as he went over. I turned away, but his dying scream smote my ears.

I walked inside, leaving the glass balcony door open. This condo had once been a haven of love for me. Now it was an evil lair, but devoid of its monstrous master. I took a last look at it, imprinting it in my mind. I don't know how long I stayed there, but, when I left, I was calm again. Gill's death had been vindicated.

I used the service elevator to leave and exited the building through one of its rear doors. Walking in a two-block circumference, I again reached the restaurant where I had waited. People had gathered across the street around Derrick's body, and the police were already there. I crossed over and stood on the edge of the excited crowd.

Looking, up, I saw Zeke on the balcony, bending over. He was waving his arms. He had to have been on the way up to Derrick's as I was descending. Now he was in panic.

I tugged at a young police officer's arm. When he looked at me, I pointed to Zeke. The officer yelled at a second officer and directed his attention to Zeke. Then the first policeman ran into the building. I slipped away unnoticed and walked home. Perhaps now my head would stop pounding.

I approached Widdicombe House through the carriage house and the garden, where French doors opened into my bedroom. Without undressing I lay on my bed, the back of my hand over my eyes. Sadness overwhelmed me. Why had I not found happiness in life? Was it because I was gay? I did not think so. Heterosexuals sometimes suffered agony. Carolyn had undergone a nervous breakdown when her husband abandoned her. Oliver had committed suicide after the discovery of his embezzlement at the bank. I would never do that.

Regardless of how bitter my life was becoming, I would not take my own.

Someone knocked on the door. Why did they bother me now? I needed to rest. The family should be at church, not annoying me by rapping on my door. It opened and Kei peered in.

"Strut, you are here. Sam Zole called. H e told us about Gill Rutledge's death."

"I do not care to talk about it." I uncovered my eyes and stared at the ceiling. "His murderer has been punished. That is the end of it."

"Murderer?" Kei looked blank. "Well, Sam said the driver of the pickup was arrested, but I don't think I'd call him a murderer. Gill ran into traffic. The driver's crime was that he drove away from the scene of the accident."

"Why are you playing detective?" I sat up on the bed. "You never did have any faith in Gill when he moved into the house!" Anger welled up inside me. My temples throbbed.

"Oh, Strut, don't take it out on me. Gill didn't get off the liquor! You know that's what caused his death. If he had stayed here, he—"

"Derrick Agnew caused Gill's death!" I interrupted, getting off the bed and crossing the room. "And do you know why I went to bed with Derrick the first time? Do you remember?"

"I'm not sure if you told me, Strut." There was a hint of fear in Kei's eyes.

"I went to bed with him so that he would loan me the money to put a new roof on The Greene Room! I could have used that embezzled money if you hadn't been so damned noble!"

"Strut, you're not making sense!" Kei retreated a step toward the door. "All this has unnerved you."

Judy appeared in the doorway. She had never heard me this angry before, and her face registered shock.

"Do you remember what we found inside this lovely old antique?" I caressed the old china clock. "We found enough money there for a new roof several times over!"

"Now, Strut, calm yourself," Judy pleaded. "Don't upset yourself like this!"

"But you maintained we had to return it to the banks So righteous, weren't you?" I hugged the clock to my chest as cold comfort. It's ticking sounds seem to become louder and louder in my brain.

"It was the right thing to do."

"Please quiet down, Strut," Judy said sternly. "The children are down stairs! Mrs. Acree is seeing to their breakfast."

"Your virtuous position, Kei, sent me to bed with Derrick, and I liked it, and I fell in love with him! And, these many years later, Derrick's jealousy of Gill led him to tempt Gill to drink while we were out of town at Mrs. O'Brian's funeral!"

"I didn't know," Kei mumbled, looking away.

I lifted the china clock over my head with both hands and hurled it through the French doors. Glass flew and Judy let out a cry. The tension in me began to subside, to be replaced by simple numbness. Judy and Kei quickly left the room.

Stepping over glass, I went into the garden. I was sick of them. Why bother to try to relate to Kei and Judy? They were selfish and did not give a damn how I felt. I looked at the beautiful blooming roses in the garden. Claire had so loved it out here.

I craved coffee and entered through the kitchen door. Because there was none already brewed, I walked into the pantry, looking for the large canisters. So much stock here. Judy could feed an army for months. Indeed, she used to do so. I forgot what I was searching for and stood there, staring at the shelves. It was one of the few quiet little corners left in Widdicombe House. I lost track of time.

Presently I returned to the kitchen. Where was Dougan? Shouldn't he be preparing Sunday dinner? I could hear voices in the family dining room. Stepping close to the adjoining door, I eavesdropped.

"I think Strut will be all right, once he gets over Gill's death," Bradley was saying. "This is a terrible shock for him."

"You haven't seen him, haven't heard him rant, Bradley. Anyway, he *is* going to get some rest. Very soon. His display of violent temper wasn't that of a well person. And there are little John and Gerald to consider, too. In his present state, Strut must be kept from them."

I pushed the door open and walked in a step. They looked at me in surprise. 1 could tell Bradley had been crying.

"I shall not menace the children, Kei! All I desire is to be left alone."

Without waiting for a reply, I left them and went to my bedroom. Dougan and Ross were there, nailing plywood over the broken panes and cleaning up the mess, We did not speak to each other. I settled down in a chair, my photograph album open on my lap.

I lingered over the pictures. One photo was of Claire, Kei, and me in the garden when Kei was twelve. Even though those were the lean years, we were happy. Another picture showed Neil and me at Ocean View. Slim and wiry, Neil still looked rather attractive in his trunks. He was a good man. Perhaps I should have tried harder to love him. Derrick had dazzled me with his masterful bedroom behavior.

Kei, Judy, and Allene Kibbey came into the room. I looked up in surprise. "We don't knock any longer?" I said peevishly. "I no longer have any privacy?"

"Don't argue, Strut," Kei directed me. "Dr. Kibbey is here. She's going to help you get some rest."

"Some rest?" I stared at them. "What I need is my Gill back!" Anger was stirring in me again.

"Roll up your sleeve, Strutwick," Allene ordered. Her face was impassive. "This little shot will help you relax and sleep."

"Did you know that Gill was my golden boy? We're not allowed to keep our golden boys very long, are we?"

She began to turn up the sleeve on my right arm, but I jerked it away.

"No, golden boys are like twinkling stars. Their radiance is fleeting!" I answered myself.

Because I had made a profound statement, I began to laugh. Then I got louder and could not stop. What a wise thing I had uttered! I had had my twinkling star. Some people never do.

Kei grabbed my arm and began pulling up the sleeve. I tugged away from him, still laughing, until Dougan came over and helped him. While they held me, Judy pushed up my sleeve, and Allene penetrated me with her needle, injecting her brew into my arm. Then they finally released me.

"Your behavior is not in keeping with my standards of conduct." I smiled at them. "I must ask you to withdraw from my bedroom."

Waking up was difficult. I had to struggle to keep my eyes open. How long had I slept? I sat up in bed and looked around. This was not my bedroom! I was in a single bed, and the room was small. It had only one window. I pulled myself out of bed, my head spinning, and went to look outside. I saw the carriage house below. I was on the third floor!

They must have moved me while I slept. Going to the door, I tried to open it. It was locked! What they were doing was illegal! When I got out of here, I would report them to the police. Wouldn't that look fine in the newspapers? The Widdicombes airing their dirty laundry in public!

If I waited, I knew I would have my chance to escape. Across the hall Charlotte had been confined. Dougan and Ross occupied her rooms now. I would simply bide my time.

The room wasn't exactly extravagantly furnished. The single

bed was iron, painted white, and a small desk, hardly more than a table actually, stood against one wall. Pulled up to it was a small wooden chair. On the other wall was a closet, its door ajar. I could see dirty clothes on its floor.

I realized that this had been Mrs. O'Brian's room. It was so like her, dear, stoic Mrs. O'Brian. No one would ever again love me as she had.

I became aware of a low buzzing noise. Was it somewhere outside or was it in my head? I wasn't sure. Just then the door opened, and Dougan and Ross came in with a tray. They put it on the desk.

"I will go downstairs now," I stated, striving to sound rational. "I am quite rested."

"No, not now, Strut," Dougan answered me, looking uncomfortable.

"We've brought you some breakfast." Ross was trying to appease me. "Why don't you eat it while it's hot?"

"Not hungry," I said flatly. I looked at them closely, looking for signs. "Tell me how long I have been in this room."

"Around twenty-four hours." Dougan had a look of pity on his face. "It's Monday morning, about ten-thirty."

"Then my family is out? They have all gone to toil at filling the Widdicombe coffers?'

"Mr. Kei is here. The others are gone," Ross said. "I can tell him you want to see him."

"Tell him at his convenience, Ross."

They left me then, closing the door, and I sniffed at the food. I decided to let the tray sit there on the desk until someone took it away.

The buzzing sound continued to annoy me. Perhaps it was some after-effect of Allene Kibbey's sedative.

I glanced at the closet door again, and the notion struck me that this had been Gill's room. How stupid of me not to have remembered it until now! I leaped to the closet and threw open its door. Hanging there were his sports clothes as well as his clean work jeans. There on the floor were the dirty clothes he had discarded that cursed day he had gone to Derrick's condo.

Sitting on the floor, I gathered his dirty jeans and tee shirt up and buried my face in them. I thought I detected a faint trace of his body aroma and perspiration. How dear he had been—how loving and naive and trusting. The world destroys the pure of heart, and we cannot save them.

Carefully I placed the clothes back in the closet. At least I had something to cherish. But there was more! I found his work shoes toward the back. I took them out and placed them on my lap. His white socks were pushed down inside of them. I removed one and ran my fingers inside it. Desire welled up in my heart. Gill had been so appealing in his work shoes and little white socks. I longed to stroke his ankles, his feet...only one more time.

That was not to be. Never to be. He was dead, and Derrick was dead, and I was confined to the third floor of Widdicombe House. Why could I not cry? I desperately wanted to cry, but the tears did not come. The pain was too deep to be relieved by tears. It was in the core of me.

I put the shoes back in the closet and stood up. It was time for me to strike a blow for independence. I had no intention of remaining a prisoner on the third floor any longer. I would do whatever I had to do to escape. We Widdicombes are a strange breed. They could not keep me up here against my will.

Struggling to remain calm, I tried the door. I found it unlocked, and, opening it, I stepped into the hall. Dougan was sitting in a chair there, reading a paperback. He looked up as I came out.

"You have to stay in there, Strut," he said. "I don't like to order you around, but I was told to keep you there. I forgot to lock the door when I came out."

"If you say so, Dougan." The buzzing noise was louder. "I only want the tray removed. I'm not hungry, and the smell of that food is nauseous. Please take it away."

"Sure, I can do that." He got up and went into the room. "Just let me know when you're hungry. I'll see that you get something you like." Dougan picked up the tray and started out the door.

"When is Kei coming up? Does he know I want to see him?"

"Yeah. He was told. He'll be up soon, I guess."

As Dougan walked out, I picked up the chair at the desk. Swinging as hard as I could, I hit him across the back. He fell to the floor, and I fled down the steps.

Reaching the second floor landing, I encountered Kei coming up. I tried to push past him, but he grappled to hold me. His arms went around me, and I turned so that my back was to him. I raked my heel down his shin, and he howled as he released me.

I was free! Twisting towards the stairs, I lost my footing and careened head first down the steep steps. 'The same as Carolyn' was my last thought. There were no more.

**Strutwick Widdicombe
and Derrick Agnew
both received elaborate funerals.
Gilford Rutledge,
having carried no identification,
was buried in an unmarked grave.
Ezekiel Scutchings
was convicted of murder
and sentenced to
life imprisonment.**

The End

© Copyright Byrd Roberts   2003

Other Byrd Roberts Books Available

BETWEEN TRASH AND TRAMP
He was a beautiful man, a professional boxer and a father, but it also became common knowledge that he made much of his living by hustling with both men and women...

Paperback Novel   1-879194-29-5   US$ 14.95

The Duskouri Tales
A collection of "gothic" short stories that take you on a journey through a largely gay, make-believe land with unexpected and often bizarre twists...

Paperback Anthology   1-879194-31-7   US$ 12.95

Commonwealth Chronicles
Collection of short stories of Virginia, gay olde time Virginia, that ring true through the land but with that special touch.

Paperback Anthology   1-879194-74-0   US$ 13.95

Available at your favorite book store
or directly from the Publisher:

For each book, send purchase price plus $3.00 s/h to:

GLB Publishers
P.O. Box 78212
San Francisco, CA 94107

Or shop the Internet at:

www.GLBpubs.com

YOUR PRIMARY SOURCE
for print books and e-books
Gay, Lesbian, Bisexual
on the Internet at

http://www.glbpubs.com

**Print book and e-Book Fiction
by such leading authors as:**

Bill Lee	Chris Kent
Mike Newman	William Tarvin
Byrd Roberts	Veronica Cas
G-M Higney	Jim Brogan
Robert Peters	Thomas R. McKague
Kurt Kendall	Richard Dann
Marsh Cassady	James Hagerty
Jay Hatheway	Dorien Grey

and of course, **Byrd Roberts**

This book also available as a download to your computer on our web site:

www.GLBpubs.com

GLB Publishers
P.O. Box 78212, San Francisco, CA 94107

$13.95 by check or money order (no shipping charge or sales tax)

Credit Cards and checks honored.